The Other Shore

The Other Shore

Cover art by Kerry Pagdin
https://www.waywardcitizen.com

Edited by Selena Middleton

Published by Stelliform Press
Hamilton, Ontario, Canada
https://stelliform.press

Printed on 100% recycled paper

Library and Archives Canada Cataloguing in Publication
Title: The other shore / stories by Rebecca Campbell.
Names: Campbell, Rebecca, 1975- author.
Identifiers: Canadiana (print) 20250172038 | Canadiana (ebook) 20250172062 | ISBN 9781998466016 (softcover) | ISBN 9781998466023 (EPUB)
Subjects: LCGFT: Short stories.
Classification: LCC PS8605.A5483 O84 2025 | DDC C813/.6—dc23

For my family

Other Works by Rebecca Campbell

The Paradise Engine
Arboreality
The Talosite

The Other Shore

Rebecca Campbell

Stelliform Press

Hamilton, Ontario

Table of Contents

Thuja plicata: An Introduction

When I was a kid, my parents made dollhouses for a living, beautiful and precise models in 1:12 and 1:24 scale. There was an ornate Queen Anne named "The James Bay" after a neighborhood in Victoria, British Columbia, and an elegant, neo-classical house that looks like something from Kingston, Ontario. There was a four-room cottage from a homestead, with dormer windows and a generous porch. I don't know where the homestead was, but you could imagine the rest of it, green fields and vegetable gardens rolling away from the front step.

A dollhouse is a dream shared between the person who builds it and the person who looks inside. Its inhabitants never notice that the back wall is missing, and that a giant peers into the drawing room from a perspective outside of time and space. The house might appear empty, but it feels like the people who live there have just left the room, stepped out into a garden you cannot see, from which they will return only when you look away.

My parents built these houses from off-cuts of old growth western red cedar, left over from more important production, maybe lawn furniture or roofing. The edge grain they used had thirty or forty growth lines in a couple of centimeters, like it was in the same 1:12 scale as the houses. Second and third growth is inconsistent, often knotty, unsuitable for this kind of delicate work.

✦

Thuja plicata. Western Red Cedar. Shinglewood. Giant arborvitae. X'payelhp. Huu-mis.

Whatever you call it, it has a narrow range on the Pacific coast of North America, running from southern Alaska to northern California, but richly concentrated around the Salish Sea. You know it by its enormous size and its scaley branches, which turn up at the tips. You know it because its sweet-smelling wood splits neatly into shingles that survive for decades in the rain. Western red cedar is a foundational tree for people on the coast, the stuff of canoes and totem poles, of fiber for ropes, broad-brimmed hats, and waterproof baskets. It lives for centuries, but like any tree, it will fall quickly before a chainsaw and a skilled logger. Pre-contact giants are cut and bucked in the secret valleys of Vancouver island, hauled out to the coast, dismantled, shipped off, remade. In their place we have empty hillsides and roofing material. Lawn furniture and tiny, perfect dream-houses perched on green lawns.

The tree is also full of volatile organic compounds — terpenes — like thujone and pinene. They burn easily, and smell like incense. When I was a child, we brought armfuls of the living tree into our house at Christmas, to put over the mantelpiece, and hang on the doors. When you walk into a house with a woodstove burning cedar, it seems to radiate heat the way a body does, the walls and masonry warm beneath your fingers, and scented like a church. In old satellite images, you can make out heaps of cedar sawdust outside the workshop where my parents made their houses, a distinct orange-gold fading to grey as it aged. In autumn, when we had bonfires, you could throw a handful of fine sawdust into the flames, and each speck exploded like gasoline, so you felt like a wizard casting fire-magic in the darkness.

Now you often see red flags on young *Thuja plicata*, dying branches brilliant against the surviving green. It's heat stress, after years of drought and rising temperatures. Without their roots supporting the hillsides, topsoil slides into the steep-walled valleys. The watersheds degrade. When trees aren't there to shade the streams, salmon fry will overheat in the rising summer temperatures. If you remove a foundation tree from the forest, everything else changes.

◆

For years, I rented an attic that overlooked an alley in East Van, where ivy slowly consumed a Subaru Outback, until the leaves pressed flat against the windows from inside the car. By now, I imagine the vine's trunk is as thick as my forearm, knuckled with branches twisting around the steering column, slowly dismantling the engine. The attic of that house was full of squirrels, which sometimes broke into my room, chittering at me from on top of my printer. Pigeons moaned in the eaves. The walls were full of mould that crept into my books, and half the front step sank into the earth. Even in the middle of the city, the forest is close to reclaiming everything we think is permanent. Underneath Vancouver, the original streams are still running, restricted by concrete, but audible through manhole covers, if you know where to listen.

That's true of the whole Salish Sea: it's still there under our roads and foundations. Whatever you build, you must remember that, because in a couple of years, the shed you put up out behind the garage will be covered with wild raspberry and Siberian blackberry, the doors and windows locked up by thorns like in a fairy tale. The path you cut through the woods will disappear. Your footsteps on the beach will fade into the shingle and the waves. Your garden will be full of alder and fireweed. Sometimes I see this mutability as salvation — that all our errors will, eventually, be reabsorbed into the Salish watersheds because the place has always been in flux. Tides rise and fall, as do the forests, the Vancouver Island plate, and the whole Cascadia Subduction Zone. Salmon follow the streams inland, carrying nutrients that are transfigured in the guts of animals, then taken up by the roots of *Thuja plicata*, so fish find their afterlives in the branches of a cedar tree. This transformation is hopeful to me because it reminds me that all things are impermanent, and newness is always coming into the world, even if you try to build a highway over it.

But then I learned the word "Anthropocene" and understood that our mark will be visible for millennia. The logging industry, the monoculture of our farms, and the lost diversity of people and landscape have permanently reshaped our world. The settler leaves behind clearcuts and a stratum of the Anthropocene, a fine dust of microplastics, ash, and lead that won't be washed away, not from the ground, nor from our bodies.

◆

When I left BC to finish my education in Ontario, I brought C.P. Lyon's *Trees, Shrubs and Flowers to Know in British Columbia* (revised edition 1965), because it evokes home more powerfully than a snapshot, or a branch of grand fir pressed in a book. My copy has marginalia from my great aunt, who set a blue ballpoint tick beside each plant she found in the wild, with a date and sometimes a location. She found yarrow blooming in June 1972 at McPhail point on the Saanich peninsula. This is important information. I like to imagine her climbing over the rocks and between the trees with the guidebook in her hand, naming the plants she saw. Yarrow. Drummond's Rock Cress. Snowberry.

You can find *Thuja plicata* in the pages of C.P. Lyons's book: here are its branches, the shape of its needles, and the texture of its bark. Not its scent, but I can conjure that myself, the way I can remember the diesel smoke of a chainsaw on a morning in January and pale sawdust falling from a gash in the tree's trunk. You can feel Lyons's affection for the region's plants in the detail he offers and the care he takes with his descriptions and illustrations. Of *Thuja plicata* he notes, "Fallen trees remain sound after 100 years" and "the largest red cedars grow on Vancouver Island [...] One 13'6" in diameter and 875 years old was cut in 1948 near Comox." I want to know what became of that medieval tree. It might still be around somewhere: a roof, or an Algonquin chair, or a set of steps running down to the beach; a doll house or an interior door.

◆

The houses my parents built look like the dreams homesick settlers might have in their new country, when they were lonely for something familiar: the shieling on a western Scottish island, the sandstone cottage from southern England. When we left the old world, we brought the idea of home with us and we set our foundations in a stranger's earth, put up four walls made of new and unfamiliar trees we found at hand, guided by our memories of another landscape in another century. When you call yourself a settler, you define yourself in negative terms: not indigenous, but also not imperialist. You say you've settled, tell yourself that the argument is finished, the conflict resolved, and now you're home. Maybe. Maybe that's why the settler landscape is necessarily strange, because we deny the imperial forces that carried us to this new home, but also doubt our belonging. For a long time I worried that no matter how well I know the place, or how much I love it, I will never quite belong to it because of the history that brought me here, which is also the history of the Anthropocene.

This is true, but it is an incomplete truth, and I find myself returning to my parents' work when I struggle with it. I grew up in a house they designed and built, one that looks a little like their first 1:12 scale cottage. They raised the walls with their friends and family, and filled the interior with salvage from demolished buildings: old bricks and leaded windows and wainscoting and glass doorknobs and cedar doors from the 1920s, taken from houses torn down to make room for new subdivisions and highways. They transformed demolition materials into a home, in much the same way that they turned offcuts of *Thuja plicata* into dream houses. I try to remember that when I'm writing, and hope that short stories can do the same, making something new out of what we saved from the rubble. The best form I've found for this salvage work is speculative fiction, which unsettles our certainties and makes the everyday unhomely to us, offers us new futures and the long view of history, human or geological. The speculative stories collected here celebrate change, even when that change is painful, a reminder that we can pick through the detritus of the Anthropocene to find something new and strange and maybe even beautiful, if we look for it.

Story Notes

At the end of his life, Guglielmo Marconi believed that signals were eternal, still reverberating through the ether long after they passed out of a radio receiver's range. Charles Babbage suggested something similar in 1837, that every word uttered was still present in the ripples and waves of the air, if only we could perceive them. It's a beautiful idea, and I like to imagine an alternate world where lost voices persist in subtler forms, inaccessible perhaps, but still present. This story is about an echo, and the way voices reverberate in sound waves and electromagnetic pulses, animating the universe like a kind of memory. The story's heart is in Vancouver in the 1970s, in a little outpost of the counterculture based on the Egress (a real club where my aunt listened to Tim Buckley and Townes van Zandt play). Like every other town in this collection, Vancouver is a product of the logging industry, brought into existence by the combination of deep sea port and Fraser River, where lumber collected before it was shipped out to the rest of the world. This is also a story about exile in both space and time, and about a future permanently altered by past actions, culminating in a ruined earth.

The High Lonesome Frontier

Freddie Weyle in Toronto, 1902

Freddie's head rested on the music rack as he murmured into the piano keys possible and probable rhymes, slant or assonant, for moon. He accompanied each syllable with a dull minor chord from his left hand. June. Raccoon. Spoon. Croon. Womb. Harpoon. High noon. Tomb. Gloom. Wound.

The last word stuck, and a terrible, irresistible lyric formed. He droned it through his nose: The June moon it is a wound. High noon gloom of my little room, and so the tomb.

How much they loved these loony, crooning vowels. Words that turned all singers into doves, with billing and cooing that sounded to his ear — he, who had lived so much of his life under the eaves of pigeon-infested houses — like an asthmatic climax. Hoon. Hoon. Hooooon.

It was hard to write about the green fields of somewhere-or-other when he heard only infernal pigeons, the clatter of wheels on pavement, the shout of boys, the rage of drivers. Despite the noise, Freddie still conjured moon-drenched country walks in terrible songs published as "F. Wilde" because he could not put his own name to them. Songs all written for a girl in Winnipeg with a quarter to spare and a pianola in the parlor. He'd seen modest checks so far, which was why he was keen to keep the harvest moon in his heart, and so avoid his natural tendency toward moon-tombs and Cdim7 chords.

If one was to write a song about the moon, he thought, one should think of its true nature: its distance from earth, out there among the meteors and comets; one should consider the luminiferous aether through which it sailed. The number of moons expanded yearly, he had noticed, as telescopes grew more powerful, and the people of Earth more sharp-eyed and watchful. There were multitudinous moons, not just their own, but Phobos and Deimos, accompanying Mars and its canal-scored deserts, Io and Tethys and oceanic Titan.

What they all needed was a song about an observatory, signaling Luna or any of her sister-satellites, how, one day, a light might wink back at them from the dark.

He thought of the canals of Mars and its moons, or the still-unnamed bodies that circled the sun in orbits invisible to the naked eye. He liked that feeling of distance, an expanse so huge his mind ground to stillness when he tried to imagine it. His fingers found the keyboard, and it seemed that an enormous, empty space formed between the question and the silence of its non-answer —

Where does that water run? he asked, and thought of Schiaparelli's canals and the spidery Venusian webs Lowell had seen through his telescope. *Where does it run?*

Maybe out. Maybe into the black on the other side of the sky.

Vocamatic Hand-Played Recording, 1904

Six Songs As Sweet As A Garden Stream, including "Where Does That Water Run?" and "Waiting For You, My Dear" by that beloved American tunesmith, F. Wilde.

For best results, choose a Dekalb pianola!

Lily Gibbs, 1898–1980

Vocals and autoharp. Best known for her signature song, "Where Does that Water Run?," an Appalachian ballad of uncertain origin, recorded ca. 1929. Advertised by OKeh Records as "The weirdest melody that ever stole out of Tennessee."

Lily Gibbs Plays the Exit Club, 1975

The parking lot behind the Exit only fit three cars and it was full, so Pat squeezed her Volkswagen behind the dumpster and knocked on the door to Ken's office. By the time Ken let her in she'd smoked her second cigarette down to the filter.

His eyes were tiny and red-rimmed. Pissholes, her father would have said, in the snow.

"Thanks, Patty," Ken said. "You have no idea how grateful I am." He leaned in close. "The vibes, man, the vibes. The woman is a menace."

"I'm lending my car to a menace? What is she going to —"

"A reactionary kind of a menace, not the kind who's gonna wreck your car. She needs to go to church, or buy a new hat or something. She hates me already — hates drunkards, that's what she called me — and weed, and cocaine too, I assume. Though it hasn't come up." He barked, or maybe laughed. "If she wasn't Lily goddamn Gibbs I'd've locked the door."

That was when she heard Lily on stage. "Where Does That Water Run?" Lily goddamn Gibbs might be past seventy, her voice reedy, but she still possessed that quality Pat had first encountered when she was a kid with a crystal radio set, listening to the air in the middle of the night. Some January evening she had put the little beige earpiece in and slid the spring along the wire until she heard a melody in the static: Where does that water run? Lily had first asked her when she was eleven. She had not yet answered, though the inscrutable question remained in her mind.

On the wall beside the entrance someone had tacked up the poster: an ink-lined Lily Gibbs cradling her autoharp, a face all tight-stretched skin over sharp bones and hollow shadows, her eyes huge and dark. The Exit Club. $2.50 weekdays. $3 weekends.

Pat wanted so very badly to say something, maybe about the crystal radio set and the beauty of a song emerging from the sheets of static. "It's really pretty," was all she could think to say while looking at the poster, her voice a shade too bright.

Lily Gibbs — really, truly Lily Gibbs, of the remarkable voice, of the peculiar autoharp tunings and the irresistible question — just looked at her.

Ken carried on in the silence. "Yeah, it's pretty good, I like it a lot. I like his work. She'll just need the car for the afternoon, is all. I can't thank you enough, Patty, I really can't. You're on the list. Forever. I'll put you on the list forever," followed by the humorless bark.

In the alley, Pat unlocked the Volkswagen, handed Lily Gibbs the keys, and took in her incongruity, so much more obvious in daylight. She wore a lavender double-knit suit with slightly dingy white buttons and piping. Her hair had been teased into a tower of setting lotion and Final Net. As though she didn't notice she was being watched, Lily took a rat-tail comb out of her purse and scratched her scalp. Pat thought of the hostess at the first place she'd ever worked banquets, whose elaborate hairstyles were set once weekly, and who was otherwise trapped beneath them, and scratched the same way with her rat-tail comb when she still had a day to go before her shampoo.

For her part, Lily glanced from Pat's head to her feet and back again to her eyes. It felt a lot like going down to the Legion to collect her father on a Saturday afternoon, with the Legion wives looking over her jeans and her long, undressed hair and her sandals with that same glance, from inside the same lavender double-knit suit and fearsome bouffant. The same oppressive censure, but this time from Lily goddamn Gibbs herself.

Later that night, Pat got the Volkswagen back with an empty gas tank and a strong scent of lily of the valley. She slipped in past the dumpster, along the corridor to the storeroom, and emerged behind the bar, where Ken was standing, his hands pressed flat on the scarred wooden top, his TEAC reel-to-reel beside him.

Lily Gibbs was just taking the stage in her kitten-heeled pumps, accompanied by men in neat ties and dark suits a little shiny at the seams. Pat's mind went again to the Legion, collecting her father from the smell of stale beer in old carpeting and a still basement room shut up tight against the summer heat.

Then none of that mattered, not her immediate mistrust of middle-aged men in dark suits, nor the disapproval from the woman on stage. None of that mattered because Lily Gibbs opened her mouth and sang for a ninety-minute set that ended the only way it could end, with the terminal question: Where does that water run, poor boy? Where does that water run?

The song began with a fairly conventional bluegrass arrangement, a lot like the 1950 recording, Pat thought, but then the instruments dropped, and their voices rose in a capella discord, the guitarist's baritone, the bassist's tenor. A full octave higher, Lily Gibbs carried a lonesome countermelody.

Then the bottom of the stack dropped out as well, and it was only Lily repeating the question: Where does that water run? Where does that water run?

The last long vowel lengthened into a drone, so pretty soon there weren't any words, just a restless sort of pain. It was like the sound had found some sympathetic resonance inside Pat at a confluence of bone, and so her eardrums shuddered like she was resting her head against an overdriven speaker. The sound conjured darkness, a limitless space on whose edge she perched, and there was nothing but Lily's half-gone voice, and a feeling inside like a rupture. There might have been a trickle of blood in her ear. Burst vessels in the whites of her eyes. The vertigo of a sudden change in blood pressure as she found herself standing.

She felt like she was looking up into the black. Or maybe it was down into an equally black abyss. It didn't matter which, because the black surrounded her. She might sense other things — a shitty underground club in Vancouver, the streets around suffused with cut grass, or blooming trees, the cold snap of winter ozone — but it was the black that mattered, empty black with all the tiny windows of the world lit like stars. Above them sailed moon after moon, through the entombing darkness so vast it stilled her beating heart, slowed her mind to a tick like a clock, then slower even than that.

Pat Makes a Mix-Tape for Her Daughter, 1991

There's the sound of audiotape first, that familiar low hiss. There's a crackle, then what might be a mandolin. Someone, somewhere, a long time ago, resets the turntable from 45 to 33 ⅓, and there's the skirl of sound decelerating. Then Lily Gibbs:
Where does tha — tha — tha —
Sometime, long ago, Pat nudged the turntable's needle.
— that water run?

In the Black, 31 Years after Egress, 2087

What do I miss? Gravity, mostly. I miss gravity and oranges and baths. I miss outside, as an operative concept. We're never outside in any meaningful way.

I miss information, which in retrospect is the biggest surprise. If you'd asked me when I was a kid I'd've thought, you know, interstellar travel, generation ships, they must know everything. I miss the old kind of Faustian, compulsive collection of stuff that used to happen because there was always room for more. I'm old enough to remember Google and how many terabytes of data I kept just because I could.

But it's amazing how vulnerable information is when your resources are limited and the infrastructure is disintegrating around you. It seemed absolute at the time. Like, Wikipedia, you know? How could something so big be so fragile? It would have survived better if it had been written on those clay tablets you read about from Mycenae, the kind that tells you how many bushels of barley they grew. The kind of tablets that got accidentally baked in some apocalyptic fire, and survive because they're stone.

It's not that we've lost everything. It's just — there are gaps.

Like, for example, there was this song my mother used to sing. It was just a folk song. I never thought to look for it until it was too late. I don't even know where she heard it. Maybe some old mixtape from Grandma, the kind you used to sing along with in the car.

Anyway. I still remember part of it: Where does that water run, poor boy, where does that water run? I sang it to my own grandkid and she said that water runs into the purification system. It took her a while to understand that running water meant something different on a planet, where water runs away into the dark somewhere.

Lily Gibbs. That was the singer's name. Lily Gibbs. I can almost hear her voice. Almost. I can hear Mom singing, too.

When it makes me lonesome, I like to remind myself that it's still out there, running into the dark. The song would have been broadcast, right? Mom or Grandma heard it on the radio, so the signal isn't lost, it's just out of reach, traveling outward in this kind of envelope, a slight disruption of the aether.

So even though my mom is dead, and the audiotape my grandmother played in her car is at the bottom of some flooded city street — even though it's all gone — Lily Gibbs is still careening through space along with every other sound we've ever tossed out there. And the basic message, whether it's Lily or Marconi, is always the same: We are here.

Somewhere out there, someone — a sort of person we can't imagine — could raise their hand or whatever into space and use the same sort of tech to catch the thin, ancient hiss of a human voice, stretched to nothing by distance, but persistent in the darkness. We're so far gone now, out past the planets, in the emptiness between home and the nearest stars, and it's comforting to think of that woman, outracing us all into the black. Where, she's still asking, does that water run? Lily, high and lonesome, spilled out past the dark rim of the solar system, and into the emptiness beyond.

Ken's Nephew Remembers His Uncle, 2031

We found them in the basement exactly where Kenny left them in like 2013, in his place in Richmond. It's all sand there. You know how bad the floods hit Steveston. We were lucky we recovered any of it, really.

It took me a while to get parts for his old TEAC TASCAM. 60 series. Those were awesome machines. Uncle Kenny took that shit pretty seriously, even if he was kind of a cokehead. He must have got it in '74 or something. Anyway. I had to source parts from all over, and we finally got it working and you should've seen the collection: John Prine, Tim Buckley, Sonny Terry, and Brownie McGhee.

I was just listening to them, thinking, *Oh, this is cool.* But then I get to Lily Gibbs. There was some nice work from Jimmy Staples on mandolin, but it all didn't hit me until the end.

I mean, I knew "Where Does That Water Run?" from when I was a kid messing around with an acoustic guitar. It's an old song.

You've heard it? No? Yeah, a lot of her work was destroyed for the shellac during the Second World War, and the masters were all recycled. But that was pretty standard back in the day. Anyway — this live performance. At first it's just ordinary stuff, you think. The microphone is a bit wonky, and maybe there was some chunkiness in his gear that night, a rough edge, even though he wasn't that bad of a tech.

But when she drops the autoharp, and loses her stack, so it's just her voice, the drone, then a keen, then a drone, you can't help but feel something, something physical. I don't think there's a word for that sound.

I met a guy doing sound art once in, like, Sweden. The performance he did seemed really familiar, like the tonal qualities he was trying to produce, something rough but kind of like hypnotic, and jarring. I spent the whole night trying to place it, and then afterward I go up to him and say, "Where does that water run?" And his face changed in that way you sort of recognize. Because that's the question, isn't it? The closest you can get using words. The closest you can get to Lily Gibbs dropping her autoharp and singing, because what good are words at that point?

I made .flacs if you want them.

Torrent Demonz, 2018

Lily.Gibbs.11-14-1975.Exit.Club.torrent
Readme.txt
LilyGibbsExitClubPoster1975.jpg
1.IWishIWasAMoleintheGround.4.17.flac
[…]
11.WhereDoesThatWaterRun.13.55.flac

Seeders: 0
Leechers: 37

3 comments

Seed pleeeeaaaase!

Seeders? My mom put this on a mixtape for me!! I haven't heard it in twenty years!

Does this actually even exist?

A Crystal Radio Set, 1966

It was Chris who got the sixty-five-in-one electronics kit for Christmas, but he didn't finish making anything, so after New Year's, Pat quietly adopted it. She opened it up on the kitchen table, kneeling on a chair and reading the instructions and tracing her finger over the diagrams, trying to understand capacitor and space age integrated circuit and wondering if she could really truly make a lie detector. She put the radio together that night thinking about how, if you were lucky, you might hear a signal from the moon, maybe. If there was a signal, you might. If you were lucky and could tell the difference between static and aliens.

The first time she put the little beige plug in her ear she held the radio in one hand and put her other hand on her lamp, and it was magical to hear the signal change, until — in among the hushing and hissing sheets of static — she began to hear something like a voice. It got even better when the sun went down. That was okay for a while, but then the lamp wasn't enough and she thought about the maple tree outside her window, too far for an exit, but she could climb it with a spool of copper wire borrowed from her father's workbench and string it in her window.

Many nights she listened to sounds from so far away they had bounced over the ocean and against the upper atmosphere, then ricocheted down from the nighttime sky and found their way to her ear. Sometimes just a voice saying, "Goodnight, folks" or, "Looks like another hot one." Sometimes Spanish and Portuguese — so she guessed — and the sounds of Pacific Islanders, the nasal accents of the Australian Broadcasting Corporation. Stations down the coast in Washington and Oregon that ran "The Shadow" all night. Once she heard the theme from "The Third Man," but static swamped the zither before the radio play began. Sometimes a thin, high tenor. Long interviews and commentaries in Russian and Cantonese and who knew what else.

Then, through the veiling static, a woman's voice.

At first all she could hear was the melody, but then she could make out the refrain: Where does that water run, poor boy? Where does that water run?

She knew she was listening not to the music alone, but also to the luminiferous aether — the phrase she had seen in the World Book Encyclopedia entry about space. It was the substance in which planets and radio waves all sailed, the deep and the black.

Freddie Weyl in Toronto, 1954

Freddie sometimes heard songs he'd written, or songs he might have written. Maybe from the speakers outside a record store. Maybe on the radio set on the windowsill of an apartment overhead as he took his evening walk. They're often in new and peculiar arrangements: "Waiting For You, My Dear" became the signature song for a local dance band, and when they broadcast *Saturday Night at the Starlight Room,* he sometimes heard it by accident, their closing waltz.

"Where Does That Water Run?" was not so common, but he thought he had heard it on the radio once or twice. Unlike "Waiting for You, My Dear," which grew more elaborate with each iteration, until it needed a thirty-piece orchestra, "Where Does That Water Run?" seemed to have become a folk song. He heard it for the last time while he was sitting in a coffee shop unable to sleep, smoking and eating butter tarts. The kid who worked late Tuesday nights that spring had a taste for folk music, and tuned to a station out of Buffalo, all ballad stanzas and old race music and banjos.

He didn't recognize it until the first chorus because it seemed to have collected new lyrics, but the song still asked: "Where does that water run?" from the cheap Bakelite setup beside the cash register. It was an unfamiliar arrangement; though, as he reached through the composition in his mind and felt the rightness of its discordant harmonies, the thud of a guitar, the manic fiddler with the cheap bow, the woman's nasal and remarkable voice, Freddie approved.

Paying his bill, he considered telling the kid who worked late Tuesday nights that the song he was singing along with? It was one of his own. Though it wasn't, really, because it was one of F. Wilde's compositions. And who was F. Wilde?

"That song, you know," he began, then he didn't know what else to say.

"I know, it's something," the kid with the beard explained. "I have it at home — it's a re-release from OKeh Records."

"Yeah?"

"The thing about folk songs is they always sound," the kid said, confidentially, as though he'd often rehearsed the thought, "like they've always been here, and they'll always be here. You know?"

And it felt true, even if it wasn't, so Freddie just said, "Yeah, that's right," and left.

Lily Gibbs Is Six, 1904

When she was very old, it seemed to Lily Gibbs that she had spent her childhood in a house without lamps, set in the winter dark between narrow hills, where the rain pattered constantly at the little windows in the parlor.

She remembered the parlor most clearly because it was where her adoptive great-aunt kept the pianola — the huge one, flying on the elaborately carved wings of many wooden angels — that sat untouched until she found it. On the walls around it there were pictures made of wool, Lily remembered. Bible verses. Lambs and heartsease and doves.

In the enormous and melancholy dark of the parlor loomed the pianola, and she felt her way toward it, following its gleam and hulk in the rainy twilight of November. There were three pieces of music in the parlor, dusted weekly, but which remained otherwise untouched on the music rack: a collection of hymns; a march; and "Where Does That Water Run?" on a huge, ivory sheet dated 1902, illustrated with hollyhocks and willow trees, a stream at inky sunset.

Lily was not allowed into the parlor except on rare and special days, or when — as was the case today — she was alone and slipped in to set her fingers on the untuned keys. Somewhere inside the wheeze and thunk might be music, and on that day she kept playing until Aunty found her and chased her back to the kitchen.

As she played, she sensed outside the window a world so huge it slowed her thinking, where lightlessness was a substance in which she seemed to drift, as she drifted in the parlor on the sounds the pianola made. Somewhere the rain was falling, and the drops raced down the panes of glass. Somewhere the water was running, though she did not know where it went. West, she thought, or just — in the manner of a child — to a hazy place called far away, that was emptiness itself. Out in the dark, she thought, where does that water run?

Beyond her ken, in the empty stretches of the sky, rolled all the moons she could not see, filling the deep with light.

Story Notes

Some settlers arrived on the Salish Sea to found experimental communities. They usually didn't last long. There were millenarian cults, like Brother XII, or the anarchist Finns who built Sointula. Cougar Annie lived a strange, wild life, clearing land alone to start a nursery before marrying a series of short-lived husbands. All were driven by the conviction that if you travel far enough away from the center of things, you will find the edge of the map, and a blank world: terra nullius, an emptiness ready to be reshaped by your hand. "A Hole Cut in the Wall of the World" is about one such dream, run by a very brilliant and very dangerous man.

The dark watchers mentioned here belong to the Santa Lucia Mountains of California, far south of the Salish, but I have forgiven myself the indiscretion, just as I have forgiven myself for inventing a new gulf island for my story, a place right on the border between Canada and America, but borrowing elements of many real islands. The rest of it could be true. The seventies were full of dropouts and homesteaders. An anti-modernist magician could easily found a new kingdom there, if he was wicked enough to do it.

A Hole Cut in the Wall of the World

It's early September 1976.

The 6am ferry pulls in after a milk run among the other islands: Cortez, Valdez, Pizarro, Fidalgo. At sea level, the archipelago is a maze, disorienting with inlets and headlands, but when the passengers reach their destination, and climb from the government dock through the dry, autumn forest, they will find themselves on the side of a mountain ridge named Cuernos de Cabra by some early Spanish imperialist. Indeed, the mountain is goat-horned from some angles, and it is populated by those creatures, who will walk down from the rocky summit to stare with strange eyes at any human interloper.

When you look up to the Cuernos and the sun is sinking behind you into the Olympic Peninsula, you might see a tall figure in silhouette on the ridge, a dark watcher looking down on the Strait of Juan de Fuca. For a moment you won't understand what you're seeing, but when you pause long enough to grasp his height, you will wonder if he's a giant. He may be a trick of the light, a Brocken specter, and he fades as the sun sinks. Nevertheless, he is fixed in your mind now, and you wonder if he was a shadow, or a hole cut in the wall of the world, revealing what lies behind the sky.

✦

Mac drove his old VW off the ferry ramp, two kids and their gear filling the tiny trunk and the back seat. They were singing.

The older of them said, "Just follow the road, then keep right when it forks." His girlfriend — sister? — was still singing one of those folk songs with a million verses.

"How far?" Mac asked.

"All the way to the gate. You'll see it."

Mac had met them on the ferry from Pizarro, two slight figures sitting beside their mountainous backpacks, sheltering from the wind. They were headed for some unclaimed property on the highland overlooking the straits, where one could see Port Angeles and Victoria at the same time. The poet HL Davies had built his stone house on the south-facing headland and written poems praising "the goat-footed / wild."

Mac was early for his morning appointment with Davies, so he offered to drive them up the long track to the gate, beyond which — they insisted — a new community was being born, perfect because it had only been founded on the solstice. Six kids had pooled welfare checks and whatever they'd saved gutting fish. They would buy the land, though they had not yet done so, and terrace the steep and sunny hillsides below their unbuilt cabin. They would nurture a single olive tree in a pot, bringing it inside during the winter. The first thing they'd do, though, was dance and pray and sing.

"For the goats?" Mac asked. The kids laughed. *For the goats,* the girl sang out in the melody of that same, many-stanzaed folk song. *For the goats for the goats.*

They reminded him of his students, the hopeful, tempestuous undergrads to whom he taught first-year literature surveys, and he felt friendly and indulgent.

✦

He was there because he was desperate to publish a book, and Davies was his best chance. He was coming up for review in the next two years, and without a manuscript settled at some major press, he'd be Assistant forever. An embarrassment for someone like him, a bright star in every department since undergrad.

Linda had suggested HL. He had never been drawn to the man's work until the summer before, when they'd been down at the water in Sooke, and she had quoted the last lines of "Eagle at Race Rocks": "By that grace we may sometimes find ourselves here / against the wild / Our eyes split wide by light of day." She'd pointed out the lighthouse rock on the horizon, smudged blue-green by distance. He'd read the poem before, but it felt magical when she spoke it. Maybe because of where he stood, and the words had caught in his mind. "Our eyes split wide," he had hummed under his breath, like a song.

When his dissertation was again declined for publication and his papers came to nothing in peer review, Linda reminded him that Davies was right there, across Haro Strait, cited as an influence by a dozen contemporary poets. She'd even found her old copy of his selected poems, the margins full of her adolescent notes and underlining. He'd used some of the notes in his first letter to HL, beginning their slow, frustrating conversation by mail. Davies' stone house had neither telephone nor electricity. It took six months to get this interview, the weekend between his summer and autumn teaching. He was lucky, Linda told him. Davies didn't talk to anyone. He didn't like to admit how much of those letters were borrowed from Linda's marginalia, nor that Davies had responded more strongly to her words than to his. Well. He'd pay her back for that. He'd dedicate the book to her, when it was finished.

◆

The kids were still singing when they reached the gate.

"See," the boy said as he climbed out. "You showed up to help. That's like *destiny*."

Mac left them to complete their journey up the mountainside toward the goat-horned summit, while he drove slowly back toward the coastal road that looped the island, following Davies' map to a switchbacked driveway. There was Davies' granite house, built into the cliff. A grotto.

That was when he saw the girl standing in the shade of an arbutus tree, dark against the bright water. She wore a white shift that hung from one shoulder. Her hair and skin seemed — even in that silhouette — golden-brown, like the edges of September leaves. Maybe she paused to look at him as he passed and he saw the outline of her body inside the whispy white of her dress, a con-fusion of curves and sunlight that wrote itself on his retina. Then she was gone.

Davies was waiting in the stone courtyard. His clothes stained with mortar and engine oil. His hands around Mac's were large and warm and rough.

"There you are!" Hereward Lysander Davies said. "Doctor MacCauley Annan!"

Mac nodded, smiled, suddenly bashful, but HL Davies went on easily, as though used to the effect he had on young men. "No trouble finding the place? I saw the early ferry was on time. It must have been Hank's shift."

"No problem," Mac said. "Right on the dot."

"Good. Come and have breakfast."

The house rose around them, high walls grown over with ivy, sheltered corners full of geraniums and dwarf fruit trees. Bees. Overhead, a shouting bluejay.

At the door, Davies stopped and touched a stone in the lintel, a tiny ceremony. He'd write that down when he got out his notebook, the kind of anecdote that worked well at conferences, told off-hand, an aside. As though Davies sensed the observation, he said, "That's from Stonehenge."

"Stonehenge! How did you get it?"

"A student of mine was posted in the New Forest during the war. And that," here Davies indicated a pale grey stone, quite small, set into the threshold, "is from the Parthenon. Also stolen. But I'm sure the presiding spirits of those places would appreciate a little of the trickster."

Inside, breakfast was coffee from an old percolator on the woodstove, scrambled eggs, blackberries, and goat cheese. While they ate, Davies kept the conversation easy: birds he had seen, weather changes he'd observed from his station just below the house. The warming and acidification of the water, which he'd been observing since he and his family moved to this site in 1920.

"We were the only permanent residents, aside from the goats. A pleasure to see goats — they're a reminder of what entities might find a place comfortable. Tough and clever creatures."

"Was it lonely?"

"It was heaven. Hard on the boys when they got older, they liked it when we weren't alone, but as it grew crowded, one couldn't find an eighty-pound Chinook off the point any longer. Some magic had gone out of the place, despite the goats. You'll notice my poetry got quite elegiac by 1940."

"It's a trade, I imagine." The words inane even to Mac's ear. He should start. Linda had written out his questions on index cards. They were in his briefcase by the door, with the tape recorder.

"But," Davies began. Mac reached for a notebook. "One should know what one is surrendering."

Mac thought of the girl under the arbutus tree, her body through the veil of her white shift. "I met a couple of kids on the ferry, headed for the peak. I dropped them off at the gate halfway up the mountain. They're the kind of kids I teach, trying to make something different from the suburbs where they grew up. I suppose they know what they're surrendering."

After a moment, Davies said, "No, they really don't." Then he stood, walked out the glass doors to the patio between the house and the cliff.

That might be a way in. He began, even though the index cards in Linda's firm, clear librarian's hand were in his briefcase. "In 'Eagle at Race Rocks' you wrote about places where the wild overtakes us, and we're no longer walled in by modernity. Where we must admit that we aren't sovereign, but are part of —" as Mac warmed to his interpretation, he forgot that he was talking to the author of those words, not an undergrad.

When Davies spoke again, it was tersely, to interrupt. "— not precisely what I meant. One can be called to pass the threshold into the wild. Limen sali."

Mac started from his reverie. *Limen sali* reverberating in his mind, familiar and newly strange at once. He blurted the question into Davies' silence. "Would you mind if we began?"

"There are the dishes," Davies said.

"Oh," Mac said. "Right."

As Mac washed and Davies dried, they chatted easily about fishing and fruit trees. The local legends: the giant woman with a bag made of snakes who kidnapped children; the dark watchers who could be seen at twilight on the ridges of mountains up and down the coast, human silhouettes in wide hats, taller than trees.

"Most visible on a clearcut," Davies said. "That seems significant to me. I often seek them out on cloudy evenings, hoping that one day they will speak to me."

Mac noted it as he drained the sink: another anecdote, for a footnote or a conference. Cultivate the sense of intimacy with the author. Those worked well when you delivered them offhand.

Then it was ten, and after the second pot of coffee, Mac realized that he had five hours before he must leave for the ferry.

"You'll want your tape recorder," Davies said.

✦

HLD: One hundred and twenty souls are all we can know, really. Anything larger breeds specialization, then caste systems. The natural man is competent in many things, able to fight and pray and love. But with more than a hundred and twenty, we differentiate into priests and warriors. One loses the immediate relationship with the sacred, and the collective, spontaneous expression of magic.

MA: Civilization and its discontents?

HLD: It's simply a new flavour of something that began in Nineveh. It began the moment we built a city. Do you know that cities find their origins in temples? They accreted around holy places. Cities are a trace of that, a memory, the consolidation of spiritual practice — of the enchanted world — in architecture and institution. The root of all evil. If we are obliterated by the twentieth century — as I often fear we will be — we might at least return to that point of origin and try again. Perhaps some other form will arise from our sacred places. Perhaps your friends on the mountain will inaugurate it. And not a moment too soon. Do you know there's a nuclear test range at Nanoose Bay? Live torpedoes, I understand, though they will deny that the submarines are armed. Do you prefer nuclear weapons to Pan?

✦

While Davies spoke, the new book bloomed in his mind and Mac scribbled desperately to keep up with his own thoughts. Davies was still speaking —

"I have come to believe," he said slowly, "that poetry is as close to magic as we may come in this degraded world. The off-island world. And perhaps not even all poetry: song may be all we have left. My new work — the unpublished poems — explores that. I should like to hear them performed in a chorus, in the ancient manner."

New poems. Mac's heart accelerated. He'd need an editor. A handsome edition, letterpress, short runs. But his own monograph — maybe frame it with a few gestures to the Homeric hymns, and describe Davies' large, scarred hand on the Parthenon stone in the lintel, how the rooms of the stone house were both radically local and transcendent, connected to the superlunary world by the poet's hand on the stone. Superlunary. That was good. That worked. A casual reference to Mircea Eliade. He'd get it to that editor at Oxford University Press, the one his supervisor knew. HL Davies was due for a re-evaluation.

He could see the title page, his name: MacCauley Annan. He had always thought (though never admitted) that his name suited a title page.

✦

Slender-ankled Syrinx calls you.
Kelaineus. Eugeneios.

✦

"I'm sorry — what —"

"'Slender-ankled Syrinx calls you,' I said. From one of my new works."

The repetition rung on his auditory nerve, like he'd been struck. It rattled round his mind, chasing *limen sali* through the noise. Slender-ankled Syrinx. Slender. Slender-ankled. The girl in the woods, turning to watch him, her wrist through white cotton slipping down her shoulder — Pan chased Syrinx to the river, where she was transfigured —

"I'll read it to you later, if you like. When we've done."

He could bring Davies off the island and back into the light of public scholarship, with Dr Annan his trusted amanuensis, his scribe.

"Do you see the stone to your right? There — no, the little pearly one beside it. That's from the very navel of the world. Delphi. The birthplace of Apollo. Where poetry and theatre grew up around a temple. That is a little piece of the very core of the universe. The omphalos."

✦

Echo grieves. The year turns. The leaf falls.
    Dapheoneus. Agreus.
    Glaukos. Argos.
    Pitys of the golden breasts will rend her garments.
    Phorbas. Philamnos.
    Nomias. Xanthos. Aigikoros.

✦

The record/play buttons on his tape recorder snapped up.

"Do you have more tapes?" Davies asked.

"Oh. Yeah. Of course." He fumbled in his bag as his brain dazzled with plans, and through them this thin filament: *Echo grieves*, he thought. *The leaf turns.*

Then it was two in the afternoon. Then it was three. Mac started up from the tape recorder and the notes he had written feverishly as Davies spoke, looking down to see that he had filled a notebook in the hours since breakfast: sketches, too, and words, and unfamiliar fragments of verse: *Pitys of the golden breasts rends her garments.* Repeated, like an invocation. He was pretty sure he had the introduction in place, and a sense of the first couple of chapters. By Christmas he'd have a proposal —

"— I know you're keen to leave, but there's still the new work to look at," Davies said, "if that interests you."

Mac stopped his feverish shuffle.

Davies said softly, "There's a later ferry if you would prefer."

He hesitated. "I have an appointment." Dinner with Linda. She was waiting to hear how it had all gone. She'd talk it through with him, help him clarify his thoughts, type up the transcripts, and index them too. She was good at that. But he didn't want to say that. He wanted his excuse to seem more important than his girlfriend —

"But there's a woman," Davies said.

"Yes."

But the talking began again. Now about the mythopoeic imagination and the power of chant. The tape recorder again snapped into silence.

"You'll want to change that, I think." Davies said.

"Oh. Of course." Mac fumbled in his bag for another tape. Now it was — four o'clock? He wouldn't make the five ferry if he tried. Around them the brilliance of late afternoon.

"One can feel the summer ending, and we're winding down to the equinox, and the season of richness. The blackberries and the apples are best now, before the descent into darkness. The season of wild fruit, and misty orchards and the hunt. I wonder what your friends up on the mountain will think when the summer is over, and they are left in the rain?"

"I think they expect the rain."

"Perhaps. Would you like to go down and see the fluorescence? Evenings have been spectacular on the water."

"But it's only —"

— But it was twilight.

"When did it," he began confusedly, looking down at the remains of the meal he had just eaten. His brain still chanting: Phorbas. Philamnos. Nomias. Xanthos. Aigikoros.

"Linda won't mind," Davies said. "She sounds like a reasonable creature. And the phytoplankton have been remarkable this season. It's been so warm, you see. One of the benefits of a rapidly warming ocean."

"The ocean is warming?" Mac asked dumbly.

"Warming. Acidifying. The sea is changing fundamentally. I suppose we'll see it light up before the end, in the hours before it grows too hot for the human body. The last human dawn will be spectacular. Olympian."

Now Mac crouched at the base of the cliff, where flat boulders served as a boat launch, and a swimming platform. The water spilled over the lip, and his feet — now bare, when had he taken off his shoes? The stars were coming out.

"So many lights on the water now. It seems unnatural to one who remembers the old way," Davies said, and crouched to stir the water with his hands. "There, do you see?"

"I can't —"

And then, at the edge of his vision, a new luminance.

"There!" he said, delighted. "It's there!"

They fell silent, Davies stirring the waters around their feet, and in each wavelet he saw that bluegreenwhite eminence.

"Millions of tiny creatures working in union. Billions. So small we only see the mark they leave on the world, not the creatures themselves. We don't know their individual thoughts or feelings, because they matter only in congregate. But do you know they can redirect ocean currents? They feed the salmon we eat and signal the stars with their bodies." His ankles and hands were glowing.

"Do you know, I think I'm hopeful because of those children you delivered to the hill. Your arrival was synchronous with their need, and that is a sign I welcome."

Mac thought, suddenly, of Linda at their kitchen table, listening to the radio from Seattle, always clearer at night, flipping through a newspaper. He thought of the girl in the white shift, and now — had she always been here? — descending the steps to the water.

In the quiet, he could hear other noises beside the faint plash of Davies' hands stirring the still basin of the stones. A bird's tired trill in the forest above their heads.

"I missed the —"

"— Oh dear boy. You missed the last ferry. We're here for good now."

"I need to teach," he said limply.

"— There's the early ferry on Tuesdays, for hazardous cargo. 5am. You'll see sunrise on the water. But now we should complete our interview. I have more to say."

✦

HLD: Imagine being so fundamental to a place that you work in happy concert with billions of creatures you do not know. Imagine that you are part of something so vast, so elaborate in its workings, that it might as well be magic, or some ancient god with a mind so large it engulfs your own and a billion billion others. Imagine that all the tiny actions of your life — your desires, your hopes — are simply pulses in that mind. And that you may not know it, but you are the light that glows in dark waters. In the black void of space itself.

The children on the hillside are singing. Can you hear them?

✦

And I am ashen.
My head on stone. Navel of the world.
Paean. Panic. Paon. Pan.

✦

Mac was lying on the ground with Davies above him. He couldn't remember why he was on the ground. The song of a fluting bird, and the girl nearby. Davies hands were rough, calloused. Her white smock fell from her shoulder —

✦

— Davies woke him with a cup of bitter coffee. The sun had not yet stained the eastern horizon. Davies seemed not to feel either the long hot afternoon outside, nor the late night, the wine, the beer, the brandy. As Mac gathered his notebooks, he flipped through the pages of writing that wriggled under his eyes. The sunlight was a thick, dark gold. The ocean below his window — what room was he in? He could not remember — was a lurid blue, throbbing against the copper-edged leaves of the oaks that clung to the rocky wall below Davies' house.

"You look a little rough," Davies said. "Are you sure you're ready for the drive?"

He wasn't sure what he said. Grunted a yes, or something. He'd arrived in the sere, late summer season. Now the forest seemed virulently green, fresh and livid with color, though it had not rained. He had seen that lovely girl slipping between the trees, her golden skin through the white linen of her blouse. He thought of Linda at the kitchen table, coffee and cigarettes and morning weather reports, *Ms.* magazine in that morning's mail. Outside, the faded city sky. Tonight they'd order takeout and watch cheap, noisy sitcoms. Anything to escape the rattling: *Paean. Panic. Paon.*

Paen. Panic. Paon. Pan.

But then he arrived at the government wharf and everything was ordinary again and he rolled onto the dangerous cargo ferry with words still rattling in his head: *Paean. Panic. Paon. Pan.*

Linda was gone when he stopped home long enough to change. In the bathroom mirror he saw someone wild-eyed and greasy. He pulled a leaf from his hair. There must have been something in the brandy. An hour later, when he was walking across campus, a student stopped him and said, "Sir, are you okay?"

Mac waved his hand and said, "Fine fine fine."

Paen. Panic. Paon. Pan.

Then he was in the stuffy lecture room, the air humming, and he thought, why don't I leave this dying city for an island? The oceans are warming and just north of here, American nuclear submarines are testing ordnance under the Salish Sea. Find a hillside and a girl in a white shift —

When he began to recite the poem still rattling through his head, the shuffling silence grew deeper, stiller. They were listening.

Slender-ankled Syrinx calls you.

Kelaineus. Eugeneios.

Echo grieves. The year turns. The leaf falls.

Dapheoneus. Agreus.
Glaukos. Argos.
Pitys of the golden breasts will rend her garments.
Phorbas. Philamnos.
Nomias. Xanthos. Aigikoros.
And I am ashen.
My head on stone. Navel of the world.
Now I seek your wild favor.
Paean. Panic. Paon. Pan.

◆

Mac was gone when Linda got home. He'd left a stack of tapes and the recorder on the kitchen table so she pulled one out, wondering what answers her questions had engendered. They were mostly her ideas, if she was honest, and she had directed his thoughts toward those things she loved most: re-enchantment, the Cuernos de Cabra and Davies' stone house.

She'd grown up among the islands, but it wasn't until she read a collection of Davies' poetry that she had recognized their magic, seeing through his eyes the dark and empty coast, the entrancing lights of Vancouver visible when he fished by night in the Strait of Georgia. Until she read HL, she had thought her coastal world was mundane, far away from the temples and ancient cities that filled the books she read, and therefore devoid of history. But then "Eagle at Race Rocks" taught her that magic haunted the coast, too, if she knew how to find it. Sometimes she still strained her eyes at sunset for the tall figures he had promised she might see on the mountains, the coast's dark watchers.

When she was young, she'd squinted at Race Rocks and imagined the Eagle falling toward the sea, cutting that dark line between civilization and wild, which Davies had said he could trace back ten thousand years, and which — Linda had thought, as a teenaged girl — she could see written in the sky.

The hiss of the tape, then his voice. The familiar thrill:

Paean. Panic. Paon. Pan.

The words rattled through her mind. *Paen. Panic.* She opened Mac's notebook, the first pages well-ordered in his tiny, meticulous hand. But as she flipped she saw the letters disintegrate into a scrawl. Nothing she could decipher, but ancient looking: cuneiform or hieroglyphic.

Slender-ankled Syrinx calls you.

Syrinx and Echo and Pitys, she thought, all those nymphs pursued by Pan. Why should Syrinx call? Or Echo grieve? What good was it to them, when all that mattered in their stories was a horny forest-dweller whose desire always usurped their own, no matter how often the tale was repeated.

"Who the fuck wants to be a reed," she muttered, and turned the page of Mac's notebook to a new page, covered with almost-words in an almost-language. Meaningless and uncomfortable. She shut the book, but the tape played on: Davies' voice continued its intonation despite her disappointment with the same old exhausted woodland fantasies. Nevertheless, the next time he intoned those words, she mouthed them, too, and they seemed to speak from her mouth: *now I seek your wild favor.*

And this time, something on the other side of the sky heeded the call.

Story Notes

When I was small, my grandmother used to take me for walks through the woods around her home, past my grandfather's work-shop and his abandoned grader, and every car my family had owned since 1968, overgrown with lichen and blackberry vines. This wood is small, less than ten acres, but as a child it felt huge, the kind of forest in which one gets lost. At one bend in the road, there was a shady, mossy place under the cedars. As we passed it, she'd whisper to me, *that's where the fairies dance.* I held on tight to her hand and shrank away from the shadows, in case I saw one of them by accident. This confused my grandmother, because what little girl doesn't love fairies? Many years later, she traveled to Ireland and during a conversation about the fair folk, she told the tour guide about her granddaughters' bizarre reaction, how she'd been *afraid.* Ha ha. To my great delight, he responded, *oh yes, she should be.*

"Lares Familiares, 1981" is about the feeling I had as a child and the Irish tour guide's warning. It's also about the logging industry's violence against people, families, and ecosystems. The violence that reminds me of the terrible bargains and curses that appear in stories of the Fair Folk. While anti-modern magic is often offered as an alternative to the degradations of capitalism, I'm not sure the Fair Folk would be any better than a logging company for ordinary people.

Lares Familiares 1981

Mal

Mal, his mother and sisters, arrived nearly late for Granddad Thorne's sixty-fifth. Mom nervous, Mal itchy in good clothes, reading silently in the back seat the whole way over, the Classics Illustrated edition of *The Aeneid* he'd grabbed on his way out the door, trying to ignore his little sisters' incessant fighting. They were the last car in, and Uncle Billy was waiting with the door open when they arrived.

Mal heard Granddad laughing before he even set foot in the house. He was relating the familiar and terrible story of his own uncle Dave, who had died after a collision with a Douglas fir that was seventeen feet around the butt. They were skidding it down to the tracks, back in the days of steam, when it loosed, mad like an old man and defiant to the end, free-sliding to the bottom of the cut, where Dave was arguing with the foreman about that day's substandard breakfast. It missed the foreman, but in its rage shattered Dave's spine. He lived a few hours longer, so his brother Malcolm — Mal's namesake and great grandfather — could say goodbye, but he couldn't speak from inside the red mash of a face, his broken jaw, his eyes tracking back and forth across the bunkhouse ceiling.

It happened in autumn, a night when damp air doused the fires, and lanterns could not brighten the bunkhouse where he lay. That's how it was when Thorne men died in the bush.

In the dark reaches of the front room Granddad laughed.

The shiver started in Mal's gut, and rather than go in and say hello-how-are-you like you were supposed to, Mal set down the two pies Mom had him carry and slid into the covered porch to hide out with *The Aeneid* and hope no one found him before dinner.

Annie

Her arms full of birthday cake and pies, she stepped inside just as the Douglas fir snapped its cables. She felt the familiar story in her teeth, and thought — as she always did — of the moment Uncle Dave must have looked up and realized what was coming, a split second before the bone-crack.

She fled to the kitchen where she could not hear the rest of the story, just the rumble of his voice, what with the comforting noise of women washing dishes and women singing along with the radio. Children begging for slivers of the roast's dark crust in a kitchen as hot as summer, though it was October.

She still saw the long familial litany of logging-camp dismemberment that only began with Uncle Dave, when her mother looked up from where she mashed potatoes and instructed her daughter-in-law to whisk the gravy. Mom turned sharp-eyed to Annie as she set the birthday cake down on top of the fridge and said, "Where's the ice cream? Did you leave it in the car?"

"Oh," Annie said, and thought of the week's grocery trip, squeezed into the hour after work, the kids waiting grumpily, and she bitterly tired. She'd forgotten toothpaste as well.

They would attribute this to her perennial mismanagement and say something like Annie always was that kind. Even though she'd got up at five that morning to make pastry and cut little birds and leaves into the crusts. She had made seven minute icing and chocolate curls —

"You said you'd look after dessert! I knew you should have just done a plain cake!" Her voice rising. "I just knew it!"

Dad would, on principle, refuse to touch his birthday cake because who ate birthday cake without ice cream? And he'd say something like Women. Heads on backwards. Buncha mop squeezers. Mixed company, and kids, so he wasn't going to say much worse than that, though Annie had heard them all at one time or another: axe wound or dumb clunge. To everyone else — eating in silence around the chill of his refusal — her pastry birds and chocolate piping would taste like ash.

"Cake and pie," Mom muttered, "but no ice cream?"

"I'm sorry," Annie said. Fifteen minutes into town, the same back, but already quarter-to-five. The unmeasureable reservoir of his scorn, a cold always in reserve that might at any moment over-spill, and if it did — "I'll go right to the Safeway. I think it's open," she said, untying her apron. "If you could just wait for dessert —"

"— It's too late." The gravy sputtered. "Ruined," she said, which might be the gravy or the failure of dessert. Or the whole enterprise of Sunday dinner and family going back to the day of Annie's birth. "I noticed Mal didn't even say hello to his Granddad."

"I'm sorry," Annie said, again, and this time her eyes prickled.

Mal

In his hiding place, Mal could still hear voices, but endeavored to ignore the details of their stories. He tried to read, starting over at Aeneas' escape from Troy with Anchises on his back and Ascanius at his feet.

He could see his uncle Billy on the porch, smoking cigarette after cigarette, the cherries flaring and falling as he dropped them into an old coffee tin. When he paced the length of the front porch he dragged his right foot, and his right arm curved protectively around his ribs, where the log had rolled from its berth on the back of the truck and pinned him to the ground.

Twenty years earlier he would have died in camp, bleeding out from the severed artery in his right thigh. They might have tried to set his leg in the hours he had left, and feed him opium if he was lucky. Because it was 1979, though, a helicopter got him out to a hospital on the mainland where they put him back together with plates and pins stuck deep into his surviving bones, long spindles of metal that conducted the cold right into his brain.

In the front room Granddad started in on a new story, his voice loud enough that Mal could not quite ignore it.

"One of those treehugger faggots was up a tree?" — Aeneas left Troy with the lares and penates, too, whatever they were, carrying them like he carried Anchises. "I would count to three —" Three slams of Granddad's fist on the Naugahyde arm of his recliner "— and I would make my first cut, and then maybe I would have a smoke, and then I'd make my back cut and I'd give the bastard thirty seconds and if he doesn't come down on his own, I'm felling him —"

Lares and penates. Lares and penates. Household gods carried all the way to Carthage and then Latium with Aeneas, a thin line drawn from Troy to Rome.

"— And if he makes it to the ground I'm going to fucking buck him myself —"

Men shifted in their seats, worried not by the sentiment but the cursing, which the women wouldn't like if they heard it from the kitchen. Keep that kind of language for the garage and the camp, mister.

In the kitchen the 5pm news interrupted AM radio crooners, which meant supper was in a couple of minutes. Mal did not yet know it, but his mother fought tears as she contemplated the failure of her dessert. On the step Billy dropped his last cigarette and opened the door, standing a moment in the hall among the discarded shoes and piled coats, as though unsure of himself —

"Treehugger faggot going to end up like a goddamn logger," Granddad laughed. "He'll end up like Bill!"

The door to the covered porch opened, and there was Billy heading for the old beer fridge, right past Mal's milk crate.

Billy turned around. Mal said, "Uh —" and scrambled for some excuse to make it clear he wasn't actually hiding out.

But a funny thing happened, in that Billy did not ask why he was hiding, but looked down at Mal's comic.

"That's a good one."

Mal nodded. Billy was the one who'd given him all the Classics Illustrated. For this reason Billy would be — until the end of Mal's life — his favorite uncle. Just now he opened a stubby full of homebrew Granddad had put up the previous month.

"You want one?"

Mal shook his head. Sometimes there was root beer, but it was homemade, unsweet and foggy with yeast.

Billy shut the door and sat down on the other milk carton, unspeaking, his right arm limp at his side, and his crooked right leg stretched out. Mal couldn't see it, but knew that under the

Wranglers were masses of tight and puckered scars, skin knotted shut along the suture lines.

Granddad called out, "Where's Bill? Get Bill!"

Billy remained on his milk crate.

That was when Mal heard three slow taps on the door just outside their refuge. When Billy answered the door, Mal expected the usual: a bleary-eyed veteran friend of Granddad's, dragging his wife into the house because of an invitation Granddad had issued and forgotten during some night down at the Legion.

It was none of those familiar strangers. It was a girl poorly dressed for the weather, just a zip-up sweatshirt and jeans with dark patches on the knees. Her hands were balled up in her pockets.

Billy spoke first. "What's up, kid?"

"Can someone give me a ride home?"

"Who —"

"— oh!" she said, as though just remembering. "I am also cold and would like to come in for a minute. I'm looking for Malcolm."

She took a step from the ugly shadows of the porchlight to the warmer gold of the house. Mal couldn't guess her age: a regular twelve or a skinny fifteen or something else entirely. Her eyes were dark and — could it be? — whiteless like an animal's eyes, whorled red-gold and brown like finely worked and oiled cedarwood.

Over the girl's shoulder lay the forest's edge. No movement in the trees; even so, he wanted to pull Billy away from the door, and lock it tight and say nothing to anyone in the house —

"Well, you found him. You look frozen solid, kid, come on in and warm up," Billy said.

He held the door for her, his left gesturing at the entrance hall. Something nearly formal about the invitation —

"— No!" Mal shouted, but maybe not even out loud because neither noticed, and it was already too late. The breeze that attended her already tunneled deep into the interior, fluttering the pink silk roses on the table by the mirror, and on into the front room where some heavy man's voice called out, "What the hell? Shut the goddamn door!"

Too late, Billy shut the door. She said, "Thank you for letting me into your house. I need a ride."

"Where do you live? I might be able to run you home."

"I live over there." She gestured with her bony little chin. "People are weird about letting people in. That is very strange, since I'm only a kid."

Then, like the gust of night air, the girl was already in the living room. Her arrival marked by silence and a new freshness that dissipated the beef and woodfire fug of the house. Granddad surrounded by listeners at whom he gestured with his cigarette. He was a large man, thick-bodied and heavy-shouldered.

"Hello," she said. "I came looking for Malcolm. He is my friend."

Mal had never seen a girl walk into a room full of men like that, right into the middle of things.

"Frienda Malcolm's." Granddad said Mal's name as though he had forgotten he had such a grandson. "I thought you were someone else for a minute."

"Last time I was here no one let me in. I was all alone."

"Well, I don't know you," the old man said. "Never seen you before in my life."

The girl smiled, indulgent, as though Granddad was a child who lied. "Billy let me in," she said, like it was an answer. "It's good to find my way back in."

"I'm going to run her home before we eat," Bill said. "Just take a minute."

That was when Grandma — drawn by the uncharacteristic silence, perhaps, or the fresh scent that reminded Mal of Grand Fir — left the kitchen in her apron and said, "Billy, who was it —"

She stopped when she saw the girl, and her first look was to Granddad, still in his chair staring through the doorway where the girl had brushed past Grandma without a look.

Mal followed her into the kitchen, but not before he heard Grandma whisper to Billy, "Dinner's in five minutes!"

In the kitchen the girl announced, "I am a friend of Malcolm's. Billy is giving me a ride home."

Mal's mother stepped forward. "Mal didn't say you were coming. What's your name?"

"My name is Tracey," the girl said.

"You should at least warm up first. And there's lots to eat. You could join us."

Tracey's voice was soft when she answered, "No, thank you. You are very nice. Not everyone is so nice."

"If you're sure you don't want roast beef," Billy said, "we'd better run you home. You know the way, Mal? You better come along."

Tracey's smile was beatific and full of teeth.

The last thing Mal heard was Grandma's meant-to-be-overheard whisper to an aunt: "You know what kind of girl just shows up chasing a boy like that."

Annie

Annie smelled Grand Fir. It wasn't from the stove in the front room, nor the woodpile outside the kitchen door, but green and fresh, as though she had stripped a twig and warmed the needles in her hand.

How did she know Tracey? A bake sale or a funfair. At the bus stop, waving to Mal as he made his way home, or walking along the road past their house. Tracey with her familiar voice, and the kind of name she should know, with her dark and peculiar eyes that were, somehow, homely. Tracey Thorne. Old Malcolm Thorne's youngest. A temporarily forgotten cousin who had — just for a moment — been lost in the chaos of Sunday dinner.

When Billy's taillights disappeared, she returned to the kitchen and her earlier anxieties: the absence of vanilla ice cream, the way Mal always found a place to hide, and the opposing worry that he would, eventually, end up in the front room, a man like all the other men, permanently enraged by government interference and treehugger faggots.

She kept it quiet, because it was probably shameful that she, eldest daughter of a logger, ex-wife of a logger, sister and sister-in-law and granddaughter to loggers, was secretly pleased with the downturn that had left much of her family unemployed. The whole town was suffering. An American company had bought the stumpage rights and the mills. There were fewer freighters in the little port every season.

And fewer dead men. But even so: what were they all supposed to do? Go north and gut fish for four months a year. Or take up small engine repair. Or get a welding ticket. Or drive a truck. Or go to the city and work on the docks, unpacking the enormous freighters sailing in from China, and load other freighters sailing back out with all the lumber that remained on the coast, the century logs, the five-hundred-year logs.

Nevermind him, he's not our kind. We're not made for that, her grandfather, the first Malcolm, had told her when she was a little girl and asked about her uncle moving to the city. We're made for something else, and he'd gesture at the trees that rose high and thick all around the house. What that meant for a girl, she was never sure, except that you spent a lot of your life worrying.

And it meant you knew the stories. When Malcolm Thorne arrived in the valley he was the youngest and the poorest and the bravest of his three brothers, following them into the lumber-woods when he was just sixteen, having scraped together the fare to go west. He was the handsomest and the smartest too, and the day he escaped the homestead he dropped his father on the front porch with a broken nose, mother and sisters crying. He never saw them again.

He arrived by steamer and walked up island instead of taking the train, following the long trail over the mountains. It took him a week, tracking slash after slash along what was now the highway. Those nights were so quiet he could hear the salmon splashing in the inlet below him as they ran past sea lions and eagles on their way to spawn in Goldstream. He passed beneath the trees, and the raven flew overhead, and the cougars stalked him through the September evenings. Under the moon he looked up to see the trees shifting around him, heard the trunks groan as a path opened, and he — sixteen, the youngest and bravest of his brothers — set foot upon it.

The forest closed behind him. The story ended.

"And then what?" six year old Annie insisted.

"Let me ask you, girly-girl, what would you have done?"

Annie thought. "I would have followed."

He nodded and said, "Your Dad, on the other hand. He's not like you and me. We follow."

"But what happened?" she asked.

"You tell me!"

Here he rolled back his left sleeve and showed her the faint gleam and knot of scar tissue that ran from the crook of his elbow to the bone of his wrist. As an adult she knew he'd earned it at the end of a flying cable. As a child she knew he had earned it during some adventure under the trees, a battle against a foe with dark wings, perhaps for the heart of a dryad.

Dryads and scars were fine, sure, like the story of a young man lost, the forest opening around him, but what had become of it all? All his brains and courage meant was that he was the only one of three brothers who survived long enough to have kids, and all those kids followed in a litany of death: Uncle Dave first, then Uncle Cam drowned under the log boom; Uncle Sandy had become a whistlepunk after he lost his arm. And here was Billy, his insides held together by metal and scar.

Next up her own Mal, her sweet kid, just two years younger than Malcolm had been when the woods took him. If the forest opened a door she was not sure she wanted him to step through.

Mal

Mal knew he'd been afraid when he opened the door and saw Tracey, but sitting in the front seat of Billy's Trans Am (1974, Billy always liked to remind him, the only year for a Trans Am), he could not remember why she frightened him. The sky was star-less and cross-hatched by branches. Billy let the engine warm up, then they splashed down the long, potholed drive toward the road.

"Which way, Tracey?"

"Malcolm knows." Billy looked at him. He shrugged. "Silly! Go right," Tracey chirruped from the back seat.

There were no headlights on the twisting October road that climbed, curve by curve, into the mountains around the valley.

"You okay back there?" Billy asked. "Getting any heat?"

"Annie needs vanilla ice cream. It's very important."

Billy smiled. Mal could just make out his grin — cockeyed because of the scar along his jawline — in the reflected glow of headlights on wet asphalt.

"Which way, Mal?"

He could not say why he opened his mouth, nor why he answered, "Right, then take the Renfrew road." It had, in old Malcolm's day, marked the edge of virgin timber.

"Got it. Light me a smoke?"

Before Mal could do it he heard the crinkle of cellophane, the brief flare of a match and then — over the back of the seat — a Player's Light.

"Thanks," Billy said, and dragged deeply until the tension along his scarred jaw released.

"You came a long way, Tracey. What are you doing all the way down here?"

"I came to see Malcolm. It's been a long time since I saw him. I missed him."

"But you've been by before, haven't you? Maybe just when I got back from the hospital? I feel like you came by once."

"Maybe I did," Tracey said. "Maybe I said hello through the little window in the front room, the one that was beside your bed. You kept it open when you were sick because you liked to smell the air outside. Maybe I missed you."

They arrived at her corner, the turnoff blocked with a government-yellow road closure gate. Billy pulled onto the shoulder. When Mal cracked the door the sound of water roared in from the culvert. Outside their faces lit temporarily by the interior light, the scars along Billy's jawline deepened by shadows, one eye pulled crooked by the split skin along his temple.

"You sure?" Billy said. "You know there's roast beef back home."

Tracey let the door close, and there was no light but the flat grey sky overhead, and the sound of water and branches, and the wind that cut among them, and the smell — so strong now, so sweet — of fallen leaves, the resinous perfume of a young grand fir growing from the ditch's bank.

"Yes."

Tracey stood in the track's mouth. It seemed to Mal that the forest parted slightly before her gaze and he saw, or might have seen, a faint, flickering sort of light, as of fire, somewhere up the mountain.

"You are not your grandfather's child, Mal. I am happy to know you," she said.

What grandmother had a voice like that? What lost sister?

He realized he still held the comic in his hand, and without thinking he offered it to her. With a kind of ceremony she bowed her head, and took it from him.

"Not quite a hecatomb." A giggle trilled at the back of her throat. "But it is meet. I will see you soon. You might come to earn your name.

"And as for you, Billy. You will go back to school in Vancouver. You should get a job as a janitor in the meantime, and a room in an old house in Kitsilano. You will study economics and Greek literature and philosophy and then figure out you want a degree in Forestry Management. I'll prepare the way, and in your last semester you will meet a man who works for the ministry. He is mine and he will offer you a job that brings you back to me."

Billy said nothing.

She touched Billy's jaw where the scar still puckered, pulling his smile out of true. "The offering is not found wanting. The oblation is made. The door will open."

Billy knelt, painfully, his bad leg held crooked. Mal was kneeling, too, though he did not know when he had done it. It was like something in the pages of a book —

There was her rippling laugh as she added, "Of course neither was his blood found wanting, but perhaps you will be luckier than your father."

Then she was gone along the track, and the flicker Mal had seen was just a flash of wet leaf, or the red light of Billy's cigarette in the corner of his eye.

It took Billy a while to get on his feet. When they finally got back into the car he lit another cigarette from the pack Tracey had left on the dashboard.

"This is a really fucking good cigarette," was all he said on the way home.

In the silence Mal thought about how at the beginning of the Aeneid there's Aeneas and Anchises and Ascanius, but there was also the irresistible thread that bound them together, there's the lares and penates, carried all the way from Troy to Rome, who are both the familial genius and the easily-disappointed patron. Who can help or hinder depending on their mood on one day or the next, and depending on how well you honor their desires. Who are both the loveliest and the most dreadful, both the fresh cut and the scar that heals it over. The threshold god and the household god and the god of the ground itself from which you are born.

He thought of Malcolm arriving in the golden age before the wars, the youngest of three, who had been first up the long spars and into the deep valleys of the island's interior, the unmapped places. Old Malcolm — the ancient one, who belonged to the virgin forest and the age of heroes — wandered through uncut stands of Douglas Fir 140 feet tall, who was lost and found and lost again. He might be a character in black ink in the pages of a comic, disappearing into the green center of the wild.

"Do you ever want to go back?" Mal asked Billy as they pulled into the driveway, the gravel popping like gunshots under their tires. "Into the woods?"

"Nope," Billy said. He turned off the engine and together they listened to rain on the roof, the houselights glazing the wet grass, gold bars and shadows reaching toward the edge of the forest where it touched the lawn. A hundred feet in there, Granddad used to warn him, and you might as well be a hundred miles. That's how easy it is to get lost.

"Can I have a smoke?"

"Nope."

Billy lit another one. They sat in silence until Mal asked, "Who was she?"

"Don't know."

"She knew us."

"Yup."

"I was thinking about Aeneas and the Penates. Or the Lares." Mal realized he had never said those words aloud. He wasn't sure how to say them. "I was thinking about how they're sometimes good and sometimes really bad, but —" Mal didn't know how to finish the sentence.

"If you learn anything from those sorts of stories, it's that you should be polite to strangers. We better get in before Grandma kills us both."

Billy was out of the car then, but Mal dawdled, wondering if Granddad had ever met someone like Tracey, and if they had met — in town, or in the woods, in a camp or a gas station or a church parking lot — what had come of it?

Annie

It was in the house.

A reckless breeze. Something wild from the interior that defied clearcuts, that rushed past new highways and the breakneck erosion of the watershed to arrive here, and blow out their candles, and ruffle the heads of children and the hairless scalps of old men. It disordered the stack of birthday cards on the sideboard in the dining room. A slight, hilarious little breeze that now occupied every room, as fresh and cold as Grand Fir in winter.

Though Tracey was gone, Annie still sensed her, like a shadow in her peripheral, the curious stare, the eyes like oiled wood. Something in her friendly and conspiratorial grin, a just-for-you sort of smile that made Annie smile right back. How thin she had been and how cold she had looked, so Annie-the-mother wished she'd thought to send a roast beef sandwich with them. Tracey. A cousin who had once been her best friend, only temporarily forgotten. Someone for whom she'd waited, though she had only just this moment remembered her absence.

Mom called the men in to dinner, but Dad only said "Bill home? No? Then I'm not eating. You can if you want."

Of course no one else would. She returned to the kitchen, now full of potato steam, so the faint thread of Grand Fir and rain diffused, and it made her sad thinking of the wild green interior toward which the girl walked.

Without thinking she was opening the freezer door to the sound of a faint giggle from somewhere behind her, and on the shelf — right in the middle, where she could not have missed it before — an enormous bucket of vanilla ice cream.

Mal

Granddad was affably angry when they opened the front door. Five thirty, and the meal cooling on the table.

The first thing he did was ask Billy, "Where's the girl?"

"We dropped her off at her mom's. Wasn't far — just out near Kinsol Trestle. But her mom got talking and held us up."

That seemed not quite right, but Mal could see the trailer they'd visited, the gravel driveway, Tracey and her Mom waving. It seemed to overtake another memory, one of distant fire and Grand Fir, and he searched his memory, as though something was missing. He'd given her his *Aeneid*, but maybe she'd bring it to school —

Nothing happened until dessert.

Mom made a little ceremony of it, with grandkids carrying the basket of presents singing "Happy Birthday" by the light of green candles. The little kids chattering in anticipation at the thought of cake and pie, chocolate and vanilla. Maybe if Granddad felt good that day he'd relight his birthday candles and set them in your slice so you could blow them out.

Granddad did not feel good that day. He drank rye and pushed beef around his plate and then, when the lights were out and the lit candles of the birthday cake glowed, he had listened hard-faced to the song, refused to touch his slice, and finally said what had kept him surly all through the meal. He turned to Bill — who was talking about maybe moving to Vancouver. Maybe Kitsilano, where the old houses went cheap by the room — and said, "You let her in. You fucking let her in —"

"— Michael Thorne! —"

"— too late now, they let her in. She'll be back. She'll be back every night knocking, stupid bitch, knocking at all the windows and doors. Won't be a goddamn thing I can do about it."

Annie asked, "Is that such a terrible thing, Dad?"

"You have no clue what her kind is or what they can get up to. It was bad for me, but it'll be worse for you. You let her in and no way you're going to get rid of her now. You know what it takes to get rid of their kind?"

A great shove against the table flipped his dessert plate onto the floor, and Granddad stood, staggering backward. Drink always made his limp more pronounced, and he dragged his right leg from that old scar, earned his tenth season in the bush. They felt the slam of the backdoor more than they heard it, a shudder that ran through the house itself and up their spines so one of the littlest kids cried out.

He was probably headed for the treeline again. No one ever followed when he headed for the treeline.

Insulated, somehow, against the chaos, Mal slowly demolished the dinner plate his mother had piled with blackberry pie and chocolate cake, ice cream, and — because Mom still thought he was a kid — a green candle shaped like a tree. He began with the pie, which was warm, with ice cream melting over the dark fruit, redolent of August. It was the most delicious ice cream he had ever tasted, smooth and speckled black and not too sweet. He felt giddy just eating it, that ice cream, and thought of Tracey. He thought, also — where did the image come from? — of the island's interior, of a long walk through the rain toward a flickering light, and the trees all around groaning outward to make clear his path.

A plan formed in his head for next weekend, how he would get up earlier than anyone else, in the darkness of Saturday morning. How he would pack a sandwich and set out on his bike for the Renfrew road. He remembered this one time he'd seen a government-yellow gate beyond which the road curved mysteriously, and no one could tell him where it went, or why it was there. He imagined following it around the next curve where — why

would she be out in the middle of nowhere? — Tracey waited for
him.

Story Notes

The highway is important if you live on the inside coast of Vancouver island, because towns and villages are far apart, strung between the sea and the mountains. If you want a social life as a teenager, you spend a lot of time begging for rides. If you do get a ride, you don't have to go far to find the edge of the map, either in the water or the trees. Of course, you are not off the map, and those back roads are the routes that logging trucks follow because highways are the veins of extraction, whether it's lumber or human bodies. I even remember my PE teacher giving us tips on how to hitchhike safely, because she knew we'd end up doing it. This may explain why I was preoccupied with the ghostly hitchhiker legend as a kid. It's a good road story, where you're not sure if the shadow in your peripheral vision is a specter or highway hypnosis.

As an adult, though, the story grows in horror. There's this doubling that happens when you write about your past, where innocence and insight co-exist, and you recognize how blind you were to your own vulnerability. I know now what could have happened if I hadn't been lucky, and the lone figure on the highway is no longer an urban legend, nor a ghost: she is a living girl in danger. Canadian roads are filled with such figures, like the Highway of Tears in northern British Columbia. The Island Highway has its own ghosts, missing girls and women, mostly Indigenous, who hitchhiked where I did, and never came home.

On Highway 18

Jen bought a 1982 Plymouth Horizon for four hundred dollars before they graduated high school, so if she and Petra wanted to get into town for the Bino's — open twenty-four hours — to eat fries and pale, oily gravy, or drink the bitter black coffee of three a.m., it was Jen who drove. Petra rode shotgun, watching the highway unfold, and refold, and unfold again as it wound through clear-cuts. Sometimes they had a place to be, a pit party, or a dozen people meeting up at a doughnut shop on the highway. A lot of the time, though, it was just the two of them, driving four hours to an empty beach on the Pacific coast of the island, arriving in darkness so absolute they couldn't see the waves, only hear their roar at low tide, sitting under the starless, overcast sky until the sun rose.

Mostly they took Highway 18 into town, running from the island's coastal valley to its interior mountains. Everyone else did, too, as though at one end or the other something might happen, and if you missed it you would miss the only thing that had ever happened or would ever happen on the island.

Anyway, after Jen bought the Plymouth they often found themselves in town, driving through well-lit and desolate streets to the 7-Eleven, where they would buy Orange Crush and gummy sours. Their only company a few kids squatting in the parking lot under lights that turned their acne scars purple and glazed the concrete a brassy gold, all these kids with blue freezie-stained mouths.

Petra often thought about Highway 18, and about how it spilled from the empty stretches, unlit, into the parking lot, the kids, the Bino's. While Jen chatted with another long-haired boy, Petra walked through the cars to the highway and watched the trucks full of logs so enormous it was hard to believe they *grew* that way as they barreled through town like it wasn't a place, but an interruption on the long peregrinations lumber takes from hillsides to sawmills and freighters and then out across the Pacific.

The kids in the 7-Eleven parking lot knew everything that happened from one end of the highway to the other. They knew, for example, about the last girl who'd been found — the one in the ditch beside the Petro-Can.

"Be careful, man," he said, a kid Petra had known in tenth grade, "you know how ghosts like highways. Watch out for hitchhikers."

"Ghostly hitchhikers?" she asked, watching Jen and her Jesus-haired boy.

"Yeah, man! They're all over. I talked to a truck driver and he told me about this girl he picked up north of Port Alice, and she told him shit. I won't even fucking repeat it. She told him what's going to go down in like the year 2000. And when they got to the bus station in Nanaimo, he pulled over and she was gone. Like bam. Gone."

"Have you ever seen her?"

"Maybe? Like. I thought I did once, but I didn't pick her up. But if I get a chance again, I'll pick her up and ask her all sorts of shit about what's coming."

◆

After she talked to the kid in the parking lot, Petra began to watch for hitchhikers. She knew the types: northbound tree-planters; a man and his toddler Petra saw on Monday mornings; guys on their way in to work or back home again. There were kids from the university headed for the beaches on the west coast.

It wasn't until a few weeks after the 7-Eleven parking lot that she began to see — or think she saw — the other sort of hitchhiker. The first time, it was a thin girl in ten o'clock summer twilight or the very early morning. This kind might only appear as a silhouette, a girl who disappeared as one glanced down to adjust the radio.

But then Petra saw her on a long straight, when they were driving behind a truck. She knew that in the cab of the truck, a man — she was sure, always, that it was a man — had seen the girl as well.

The truck stopped. As they passed, the girl had reached the passenger door and was illuminated by the interior light, and though Petra looked back to see her face, she saw only her dark hair and the driver's silhouette in the cab. The sight was so familiar, Petra wondered if it happened every time they drove that road, every time they saw a girl stick out her thumb to get a little further down the highway.

Her mouth was dry when she finally asked Jen, "Does it feel weird to you?"

"What's weird?"

"That girl back there."

"It's not weird, it's *stupid*. Remember what happened to Nicki?"

And then the thin whine of stretched magnetic tape interrupted Jen as she was about to mention, say, the girl they found in the ditch by the Petro-Can, and talk about how they should all know better.

◆

Of course Petra hitchhiked, too; everyone did even if they never talked about it. The bus only ran twice daily. You didn't have a car. It was different on an island anyway, you all knew each other, though she was rarely picked up by anyone she knew, which meant her parents didn't have to hear about it. Things happen, of course, but when don't they? Girls are lost, then they're found again, and that's often worse than thinking they've disappeared somewhere, into the city maybe.

The last time she hitchhiked was at the end of a long day on the river in July, before she left town for university. She was supposed to get a ride with someone's cousin, but they wanted to stay so Petra started walking back to town. She still had 15 km to go — and was at least 10 from a payphone — when she decided to push her ratty, river-tangled hair behind her ears and stick her thumb out into the empty road.

A huge beige car emerged from one of the driveways in the subdivision past which she walked, right there, like he'd been watching for her.

He unlocked the door and she asked, "Where are you headed?"

"Just returning some tapes to the video place on Festubert, that good enough?"

They chatted about one of the tapes he'd rented. *The Thing*. There was one part with a defibrillator, with the man's chest opening up and the doctor shoving his hands right up inside the body. But that monster — it bit his hands off and swallowed them and then turned into something new and then something else new. He laughed. He said it again, about the doctor's hands plunged inside the man up to his wrists and bitten *right off*.

Then, halfway into town he asked, "Are you working?" And Petra said no, she was going away to school in September, so she wasn't even sure if it was worth looking, though last summer she'd got a job at an ice cream place. That had been okay.

"Oh." He sounded disappointed. "I was looking for a girl."

"Yeah," Petra said. "Ha-ha."

Ten minutes later, they pulled into the parking lot of the Video Pantry. She picked up his three VHS tapes and reached for the door. It locked under her hand.

She pulled on the handle.

"You want to go have coffee?"

"No, no thanks. Ha-ha," she said.

"Too bad."

She pulled on the handle again.

"I have to get home. Ha-ha. My dad —"

She pulled on the handle. She didn't see him move, but this time the door opened. She returned *The Thing* and the other tapes, then waved over her shoulder and fled along the sidewalk of the strip mall hoping she would not look up to see the beige Reliant and the man watching her. As she walked the rest of the way home, she still heard the door clicking shut, even though it was a sunny Saturday afternoon, and even though she was in a parking lot full of minivans and children.

She fixed him in her mind: the man with the scaly red skin along his white hairline, the heavy ring on his left pinky, the tuft of white hair poking through the placket of his golf shirt. His khaki slacks. The pine-scented beige-velvet interior of his car. The doors that lock and unlock and lock again.

✦

Not that it was the first time someone had asked if she worked. It starts early. Fourteen on the sidewalk after the movie let out, waiting for Petra's mom. A car pulled up close and the driver — some guy with a scrubby mustache and the ubiquitous baseball cap — opens his window to ask, "You girls want to party?"

Jen giggled, and Petra said something like, *Um. I don't know?* Her voice weak-sounding, the way it rose at the end. The guy pulled away without saying anything else.

"He was kind of cute," Jen said.

✦

This was how it used to be. You are both sixteen. You will be an actress. You will be a world traveler. You will direct great films, or write epic novels. You will fuck a million beautiful men. Just for now, though, you're lying together on an air mattress in a backyard and listening to a mix-tape you have listened to a thousand times already and which has been distorted by all those listenings and by the cheap cassette deck in the car, and by the heat of summer. For twenty years afterward you will keep the tape, and when you listen to it, and hear the familiar distortions that time and repetition make, it will break your heart a tiny little bit.

When you're sixteen, though, that doesn't matter, because you'll be out of here pretty soon, and mix tapes are easy to make and easy to lose.

Jen says, "This is the start of a montage. Like, the opening part."

And yes, Petra thinks. Because these are the sharp, poignant scenes that spark the story, and what begins with two sixteen-year-old girls pledging their eternal ambition and their absolute affection will, in fact, end somewhere else entirely.

This is true.

♦

But this was how it ended up happening. In July there are parties in someone's woodlot or in a gravel pit where even on a hot night the air is cool and clammy. Some girl was playing Bon Jovi and someone else insisted, noisily, on Guns N' Roses. There are two guys. Chris with the startling dark eyes and the buffalo plaid, his chin angry with pimples, drinking Kokanee or Carling High Test. He's brought a friend, Eric, whose eyes are not so startling but who is otherwise identical, down to the High Test. Eric was obviously instructed to entertain Petra while Chris chats with Jen, and Petra is aware of this.

For these reasons she shotguns the gin she stole from her parents, and is surly, and thinks, *This is just so stupid*, but Eric sticks with her. Jen and Chris move farther away, and a little closer to one another, then farther again from where Petra sits on the hood with her attendant Eric talking about Guns N' Roses, who suck.

Jen says something Petra can't hear, but she knows what's happening because she's seen it before, when Jen was faced with any number of men, gas station attendants, and waiters, with the boys in their Consumer Education class, with Petra's own younger brother. His looks were always plaintive when Jen came to dinner, with her very blue eyes, and her very dark hair, and her translucent skin, the fine, long bones of her fingers, her narrow ankles, the pale stem of her wrist.

"So, what's going on with you?" Eric tries again.

"Just. Stuff. Summer stuff."

"Cool. Cool," he says, then, "Yeah." Then, "So you hear about that girl?"

"At the Petro-Can?"

"No. She was off the trail at Skutz Falls. Don't know how long she'd been there, but someone saw her on the highway a few days before. It's pretty stupid, you know, it's pretty stupid to go out there alone."

"I guess," she says.

"I heard her neck was —"

Petra listens for a few minutes longer than she can stand about what happened to the girl.

Abruptly she has to pee, so she explains to Eric, who is like, *Um, okay,* and she knows he's happy to interrupt their conversation. Petra walks through the long, spindly shadows the bonfire casts among the trees, and though the night is very dark around her, she keeps her back to the light and pushes through the bush. She can feel around her the night that engulfs them, the deep reaches of the island's interior, its valleys and mountain ranges. And she thinks, as she often does — because this scene is not singular, but repeated that summer — about how far she would have to walk to reach the dark places of the island. How long, she wonders, would it take to become lost?

She'd walked the trail to Skutz Falls a dozen times. She'd gone on field trips there and camped with Jen, hanging out on beach towels by the river.

For a moment she hears — as though she was still in the beige-velvet Reliant — the sound of a door locking and unlocking, locking and unlocking.

✦

When she got back, Petra was happy she couldn't find Eric any-where. She crawled into the backseat of Jen's car and put her head down on a bunched-up sweatshirt that smelled of Cool Coconut Teen Spirit. She sank into the uncomfortable, paralyzed state that is necessary when one tries to sleep in the damp backseat of a Plymouth Horizon, but she did not sleep. Time passed quickly and slowly and quickly again, so when she closed her eyes, "Patience" was still playing on the tinny speakers of a car somewhere nearby, and when she opened them, it was "Stairway to Heaven." Between closing and opening her eyes she had lived only a few, fretful moments.

The night was short, though, and when the sky lightened, she got out of the car and walked past sleeping-bagged bodies in the beds of pickup trucks or curled as she had been in the backseats of cars — though not alone.

Jen must be somewhere among them, in the back of Chris's truck, or lying on a tarp on the other side of the fire. Petra decided, *That's enough, fuck it*, and wrote a note to leave on the dashboard. *Going home. I hope you had a really really really great time with Chris.* She followed the rutted driveway from the pit to the road where, under the first yellow stain of dawn, she saw a girl. It was Jen.

"Hey!" Petra shouted. "Jen! Wait for me!"

The girl didn't move, so she shouted again, and then a car pulled out of the pit's driveway and onto the shoulder. Petra glanced upward without thinking to see the stars wink out as the sky turned from black to blue. When she looked down again, Jen was gone. The car stopped and someone's older brother asked if she wanted a ride back into town.

✦

Petra tried to explain about the note, but by August Jen didn't have any time. She moved in with the Parkinsons to look after their three kids when Mr. Parkinson headed to Yellowknife for three weeks a month. After the kids came Chris, and after Chris there was Jen's mother, and after that it might be Petra, if she was lucky. It didn't matter, she told herself, because sometime soon Jen would call. They'd escape together in the car, and if they saw a girl hitchhiking, Petra promised herself, they'd pick her up. She would make Jen do it, before it was too late.

Jen never called. Petra finally caved on the last weekend before she left for university, and Jen agreed, if reluctantly, because she had to work six days that week, and it was going to be Chris's birthday soon.

They drove for two hours to an empty beach with a spiral slide and a tire swing. They ate jelly worms and drank Orange Crush and drove home just before sunrise. Petra saw the girl first. She was a slightly darker shade of gray than the predawn highway.

"Let's pick her up."

"What? No. Do you know her?"

"Just once? Okay?"

They reached her, their headlights sliding across her pale face — the dark hair, the skinny limbs in denim — and Jen, still bristling, pulled over onto the shoulder.

Petra opened the door and got out.

"Hey!" she called back. "You need a ride?"

So quiet on the shoulder that when she heard a crow overhead, she glanced up. When she looked back, the girl was gone.

Inside the car, Jen rested her head on the steering wheel. "I need to sleep," she said. "Hurry up."

"She's not there."

They drove on in silence, Jen's knuckles white, her eyes fixed. When they reached Petra's house, Petra said, "You don't want to go for breakfast?" her voice plaintive in a way that surprised her.

"I have to work in, like, two hours."

"Do you think she looked like you?"

"No."

"I thought I saw you before, once, that night at the gravel pit. You were hitchhiking."

"Why do you keep —"

The last word cut short in a sob. Petra got out of the car. The last thing she said to Jen was, "Will you come visit me, maybe?"

"I don't know," Jen said.

"You could come visit," Petra said again, and even she could hear how plaintive her voice was and knew — without Jen saying anything — that the answer was *no* because who would pay for the ferry?

◆

Petra didn't call and Jen didn't call and by the end of the week whatever had happened between them, it felt final. Petra was going to say something, but she'd wait and find a cool postcard from some bookstore on the mainland. She'd write a real letter. Or maybe next time she was home she'd phone, or they'd run into one another downtown. It was stupid not to call, but the longer she waited, the harder it was to break the silence.

When her parents drove her to the early ferry on her last day as an islander, it seemed to Petra that girl after girl stood on Highway 18. The fading moon cast long, uncertain shadows occupied by girls who reached out into the darkness to flag down a car that might take them away.

"Could we stop for her?" Petra asked, pointing at a distant figure.

"I don't see anyone," her mother said, and when Petra looked again the highway was empty.

◆

In the end, this was how it happened.

Petra spent the summer after university lying on the bleached grass of her parents' yard with a yellow-paged paperback falling open on her stomach. When the silence got to her, she drove into town. She talked to the kids at the 7-Eleven, and shared a freezie that glowed an atomic pink. She was invited to a pit party, and saw the logs still leaving the clear-cut valleys. A girl had been found out behind the garbage dump.

At twilight on an empty stretch of highway, headed home, she saw the girl. As she pulled over, the evening felt so familiar it might be the reenactment of something that had already happened, or maybe a meeting she had arranged and forgotten. She glanced back into the darkened east, away from the fringe of green sunset — maybe to give the girl her opportunity for escape — but the girl was still there, making her way toward the car. Petra opened the door and said — as though they had rehearsed it — "Do you need a ride? Where are you going?"

She was careful not to take her eyes off Jen. In the twilight she looked no older than she had four years before, or five, or however long it had been.

Jennifer did not speak. The sunset fading, and the stars emerging, and Petra remembered again how dark night could be.

"I'm on Ypres," she said, "right on the corner near the school."

They drove in a musty kind of silence, Petra's eyes fixed on the empty road, darker and darker until the world outside her headlights vanished.

"What happened to the Plymouth?"

"It broke down after a year or two. The Parkinsons let me go, and Chris had a car, so you know. He drove me around."

Petra wanted to say how sad she was about the Plymouth. She wanted to talk about how she was really considering going back to school for library science or something. Or how she could get an internship or teach English overseas. There was something confessional about the night, something in the smooth passage of concrete beneath their lights and the sky overhead darkening.

It was full dark, proper dark, by the time Petra pulled into the little gravel drive off Ypres and finally said something true.

"I miss you."

The voice that responded was drowsy and flat, not much like Jen's at all, but what it said had the quality of a prophecy: "That is true, as far as it goes. One thing you need to remember: for you it was always going to be different. You will teach English in Korea. You will cry in front of a pho stand in Hanoi. On a beach in Crete you will fuck a boy whose name you can't pronounce. You will come back here the autumn you turn thirty and, when you are cleaning up your old room in your parents' house, before they sell, you will find a box that contains your old report cards, and the star-shaped notes we used to exchange in tenth grade, a card I gave you for your sixteenth birthday, and you will wonder where I am, and you'll go into town and ask around, but no one will know. They'll remember the last time they saw me, and think maybe I headed for the mainland after I broke up with Chris. My mother will have moved, and when you call her number — which was my number, and which you will remember to the last day of your life — a stranger will answer."

Somewhere, Petra heard the sound of a door locking.

"You won't know what to do, exactly, and people disappear all the time, and I seemed pretty smart. Not like those other girls, you'll think, though that won't be true, either. I am exactly like those other girls. All of them."

"Jen —"

But Jen was gone. At first it felt so silly that Petra looked in the footwell, and the backseat, and through the window.

She got out of the car and walked across the gravel to the cottage with its unpainted trim, and the asbestos shingles a dull green, moss. Somewhere, the incessant barking of a dog.

As she was hesitating, the front door opened, and there was Jennifer. The dog barking inside the house, louder now.

Somewhere a man shouted, "Who is it?"

"It's —" Jen began.

Petra cut her off. "Let's go somewhere. Let's go to the Bino's. I'll buy you all the fries and gravy you can eat. I'll buy you the big order." She knew it was stupid to say out loud, but she went on, "We'll listen to mix tapes and we'll go to the beach in the middle of the night. We'll go now. I'll buy gummy worms. I'll buy freezies."

"What are you even doing here?"

"Please," she said, "just come out for a drive."

That was the last she saw of Jen, as the dog started barking again, and the door closed, and the light inside the cottage went out.

I wrote this story while looking at maps of radiation leaking from the Fukushima reactor disaster, making its inexorable progress across the North Pacific. So it's another story about distance, though in this case that distance is also about time as well as space, about what Vancouver Island was in the deep past, and what it will become after nuclear disaster and climate change.

There are some really good local legends on Vancouver Island. You hear about the remains of a Spanish monastery lost somewhere in the woods north of Leechtown, where the old adits are hidden by undergrowth, and if you're not careful, you'll find yourself at the bottom of an abandoned mineshaft. You could discover the writing of a shipwrecked Chinese sailor of Hui Shen's company, the last survivor of that Tsi dynasty voyage in search of Fusang. Maybe you could find pottery left by a fourteenth-century Japanese sailor shipwrecked on the east-bound North Pacific drift. Or further back, to the first Eurasian arrivals, traveling down from the Bering land bridge during the age of megafauna. If you follow a deer through the undergrowth and leave the highway behind, you will find sasquatch and cannonballs, sure, but maybe someone even older. Someone who's been here for millennia, watching the continents drift to their current positions. Whoever they are, you should probably remember the best advice from fairy tales: always be kind to strangers.

The Other Shore

The shoreline is indefinite, having been closer to the village, or across the bay, or far out in what is now a channel. For a few hours on a day in 1700 it was a kilometer up the river valley. I know this because I remember the day in 1700, but if one is shorter-lived — or not so clever — one might know that temporary high tide by the stumps that still stand just short of where the ground rises, exactly as they did on the afternoon of the tsunami. It's a ghost forest now, and runs all along the river, so far inland that when one reaches its edge, one can no longer hear the waves.

Every summer for a decade now, Charlie brings a gang of them to town. They change year to year, students mostly. In other years I ignored them, maybe said *hello Charlie* when I passed him on the street or in the restaurant.

This year, though, their dig takes in the midden. Do you see the grey heron poised above his supper, where the beach is the white of discarded mollusk shells? That is a human undertaking, and nearly as old as I am. Its history does not instantly reveal itself to short-lived creatures of Charlie's kind, and in ten thousand years there has been little change in the whorl of the periwinkle, or the abalone's deep and iridescent shell. Someone pried them open. Someone cut the muscly foot that anchored the hinge, and ate its body, and discarded its shell on the heap. If Charlie climbs up the hill from the midden, into town and the restaurant, I'll serve them a similar creature garnished with lemon wedges or wrapped in a cone of irradiated nori.

Charlie's crew brings trowels and huge spools of high-visibility twine. They bring the laws of stratigraphy that fix time and its progressions in place by measuring the earth below their feet. They segment the ghost forest and dig up flat spangles cut from mother-of-pearl, chips of obsidian from a quarry eight hundred kilometers to the south and far inland; a dusting of volcanic ash, and the denser, blacker deposits of a forest fire.

They don't often know what they're looking at, though their work is meticulous. Even Charlie misses evidence of the other shore: ancient tree-roots sunk in the unforgiving salt. Palm fronds. They find but do not recognize the tooth-chip from a shipwrecked sailor who left a village outside of Quanzhou during the reign of Gegeen Khan. Filaments of rope from an outrigger canoe. A Tahitian pearl. They find a glass float — faintly blue-green, as though constituted in the water from which it emerged after decades mid-Pacific, passenger on a March storm of 1930 — that belonged to Susumu, a Meiji fisherman.

◆

In the afternoon the sun throws long shadows toward the beach, and Charlie leads them up the hill from the dig to the restaurant, where they take one of the big tables on the sidewalk. I make sure they're in my section, so I can listen, and say, "Hey guys, I'm Lin. I'll be looking after you," and bring them pitchers of Sea Dog Amber Ale. One of the younger men talks — uninterruptible — about microbrews until I don't know how Charlie stands it.

I bring them calamari and the aforementioned sweet abalone (imported, having been fished to near-extinction twenty years ago). Chips, deep fried mac&cheese, sashimi (the salmon is farmed, the snapper is not), mercury-rich tuna tataki. Extra napkins. I know what they want before they do, in the manner of one who serves with great talent.

"So, what did you guys find today?"

The girl with the unwashed hair says, "Some rope fragments. A glass float."

"Those are so pretty!"

"*Pretty.* Okay." Corrected by the young man who cares so much about microbrews. He's the one who explained to me, the first day that they are *archaeologists.* He is an *MA Candidate.* He works on *pre-contact material culture of the Malahat Nation.* I think of Susumu, and how he lost the five floats his uncle made when he was little, that he inherited from his father the season before. How four shattered while this one survived the Pacific gyre to alight here. Unlikely. "They're for *collectors,*" he adds.

"They're nicer than Styrofoam, that looks so awful on the beach. We're doing a great oyster burger today."

"How's the halibut?" Charlie asks.

I look for my manager. She's distracted.

"I wouldn't, if I'm honest. But the chowder is awesome." I think about immigrant cattle from Jersey, and the long migrations of saffron. Their unlikely collision with bacon and scallops at this far western margin. They order the chowder.

From the sidewalk we can see most of town, hear the sharp, sweet echo of footsteps on concrete at the bottom of the street, where the kids are now emerging from the afternoon, caped in beach towels, their parents laden with coolers, laden also with radiation and its malignant gleam. On my way to Charlie's table with ketchup bottles and malt vinegar, I stop to watch the kids climb toward the ice cream shop and wish I could tell them to fill their mouths with seawater and then order a double cone, so salt might render the ice cream sweeter than anything that has ever existed.

✦

Their first opportunity came in the form of a button that unsettled their stratigraphy. I felt the frisson when they found it, spreading through the six as though through a single body, and I knew they had touched the other shore. I thought, *maybe it's time.* I was hopeful.

The button arrived on the waistcoat of a very young midshipman-and-water-colorist who leaned over the gunwale of the longboat in which he traveled from the HMS *Encounter* to an earlier iteration of this very village. Under the water he saw an even earlier village, drowned, though he could make out the fallen poles of a longhouse, and was contemplating its age when he realized that a face returned his gaze. It was a whale, perhaps, or a thunder-bird carved in wood, with a few grains of paint still affixed, showing the eyes staring upward. An amnesiac ancient, he thinks, god or *genius loci* dozing among the dooryards of what was once a village, that squatted on what was once the shoreline, before the glaciers melted, the waters rose, or the land fell.

The watercolorist is not a good sailor. His uniform is in bad repair, and one button of his waistcoat rests against the gunwale as he reaches down to the surface through which he looks — past his own eyes, which make anxious contact with their doubles, as though in warning — and down to the other shore, just out of reach. He leans, dirtying further his dirty cuffs, and the indifferent stitches of his last mend break and the button springs over the gunwale and into the water and *clops* like a stone that won't skip. The old creature, the amnesiac, reaches out one hand to catch the falling button to its bosom.

That's gone, then. Back onboard HMS *Encounter*, he'll be admonished for his disgraceful appearance. Behind him the button remains, covered in silt, then in sand, then in a plastic baggie with a tag in Charlie's terrible handwriting. He keeps it in his pocket because it confuses him. It is a disobedient button. It undermines known laws regarding the deposition of strata, and the careful exhumation of the past. It is only the beginning.

But before that, and just this moment, the longboat surges toward the shore and the *arboreal haunting* stands knee deep in yellow grasses, the midden white at its feet. The midshipman cannot imagine it, but there was once an enormous wave, rising through the shallows until it curled over the low bush of the shore, and rising through the villages it dragged the children out to sea, sending them all down to the other shore.

✦

If Charlie's lot were the kind who had prophetic dreams, and if it were among my talents to provide them with prophetic dreams I would send them this. I would have one — the girl who doesn't wash her hair, perhaps — awaken in a longboat, or a kayak, or a canoe. She would look down to find herself wearing a skirt of cedar bark. She would lean where the watercolorist also leaned, and see the drowned world, the faintest, whitened outline of its foundations, a glimpse of stainless steel through the seaweed. Or — if I am ambitious, and trust her to understand — the gleam of something that does not yet exist from her perspective: an underwater bulb attached to a surviving solar panel that still works, sometimes, despite the microbial haze of seawater. In the manner of dreams, she finds her eyes zooming in to see, beside the panel, a cellphone lying on the ocean bed, where no such thing should exist.

✦

The next day my feet hurt before I'd even put on my black nurse's shoes, and the hot oil of the fryer had so penetrated my work skirt that it stunk — like fish, like fryer grease — even as I pulled it off the morning laundry line. And I thought, *I will never not smell of fried fish, even if I live another ten millennia, even if the Kula plate rises again like Lost Atlantis. Even if the radioactive plume re-collects itself, and the glaciers return with the thunderbirds and abalone.* I remember smelling of smokehouses and doghair, and before that of mud and green things, but never so inescapably as I do now.

That is the day — when I cannot stand the humanish smell of my awful black polyester work-skirt — that they come into the restaurant carrying a yellow Sony Sport Walkman, filthy, from 1986, and set it on the table.

"Oh, hey," I say pointedly, "do you guys want a towel for that?" And when they don't answer — rendered giddy and stupid by the object before them — I bring them bar towels anyway, with which they do nothing, preferring to stare at the Walkman as it leaks ash onto my nice red plastic tablecloth. Though they found it under the deposits of a pre-industrial forest fire, it is still brightly yellow. Inside there is a mixtape from 1987 whose second side is made up entirely of "Heaven Knows I'm Miserable Now" repeated six times.

"We've got some awesome specials —"

"— Charlie, it's a *hoax* —"

"I'll give you some time," I say, but Charlie calls out to me, over his shoulder, waving his hand as though I'm a taxicab. It would only be worse if he snapped his fingers.

"A couple pitchers of the lager, eh?"

"Yeah, yeah," I say, "on their way."

✦

The next morning it rains. When I've finished with the ketchup bottles, I go out back through the kitchen with bag after bag of trash — dirty napkins, and child-gnawed straws from lunch, the fragile shells of shrimp with their powerful stench. In the parking lot, which is puddled and oilslicked with rainbows, I think about them under their tent, washing the fragments that so obsess them. These tourists, who reach their hands for the other shore without knowing a damn thing. These temporary souls, trespassers, immigrants, how immune they remain to unlikelihood.

They will find or have found the anklet of a Tuamotuan woman who reached this blue-green shore by a series of tragedies and accidents I alone remember. She arrived in an outrigger, blown from the far western islands, four months pregnant, her skin caked with salt and her eyes fluttering in their sockets, but the little swimmer in her womb turning his somersaults, and kept safe in his own seabed of salt and blood. I brought her water, and fed her salmon and salal berries from a cedar bowl. She bore her child. She died twenty-five years later, left five children, and her anklet in the earth below a longhouse whose remains are now halfway across the bay. A black Tahitian pearl, a bead of polished lava, and another of island coral that shed a faint light — diffuse, atomic, tropical — from the atoll of its birth.

They'll find the pearl. They'll find the stone from five thousand years before, that a young man strung on a line of tendon and flung out across the bay, and promptly lost, the silly boy, though it was my gift to him, when he needed it.

✦

That evening, I brought them three pitchers, and then another three, and they drank under the awning while the rain fell. The first prescient bronze on the maple leaves, hinting at autumn in high summer.

"So, it's contaminated," Charlie says, his greasy grey hair hangs in elfknots to his beard. He is remarkable for the constant dirt beneath his fingernails, the nervous flutter of his eyes.

"But the sedimentation —"

"— Sure. Fine. But there's a coke bottle in a strata of archaic cedar ash."

Charlie has made it clear that he will not be taken in because Time's voyage is one-way — even in a Tsunami — and he is blind to the tangled logic of the high tide line. When I ask if they want to try the banoffee pie we've got on for dessert, he ignores me, and that's *childish*, Charlie, I thought you were better than that. You're just *rude*.

"Okay. You want coffee?"

Charlie snaps his *no* so sharply it might be a door slamming, and then I think back at him *what do you take me for, little monkey?* But he is impervious, so I lean on them with my own sharpness. They're too stupid to feel their minds ripple, to notice that the slammed *no* opens into *yes*. In the kitchen, I collect mugs on a tray, and I breathe over them, and over the sugar packets, the cream, covering all with the faint and invisible film of my breath. Salt.

◆

It will swamp you with the smack of saltwater, especially you, Charlie, in the instant your lips touch the lip of the cup that has upon it the salt of my mouth. You will find yourself unable to stop thinking of the moment your head goes under, how for an instant your scalp is dry under your hair, before water winkles through to the roots and your skin leaps to goosebumps, and then submerged you tilt your head and seawater is in to your eardrums, and your sinuses, and down your throat, and all the wrigglers, the drifters, the spunk, the free-floating ovum, combining into the drifting zygotes of a billion different creatures, the single-celled and the amoebic, microbial colonies and embryonic clusters. Charlie. The salt stings inside you, as the water carries all those creatures up into your skull, before you release them in a snort and a bloom of mucus. You're tumbling and buoyant in the cold and the salt, a blue-green element constituted in bodies fucking, and dying, and being born, and growing, and leaving behind their recombined genetic matter to further recombine.

For an instant he is a drowned man. He rouses himself long enough to pay the bill and trail after the others up the hill to the guesthouse. He knows that somewhere there's a trigger, but he's too stupid to remember the taste of my breath in his coffee. That evening, the setting sun glanced between the edge of cloud and the horizon. For a moment, the air was cool-smelling and wet, as it will be in October, when the tourists are gone, and only newly-drunk teenagers will still go swimming.

That night some of Charlie's crew will creep into bedrooms not their own, carrying condoms and bottles of brandy. The tedious young man who so loves microbrews will smoke a cigarette in the gazebo at the bottom of the garden, the one that overlooks the wetlands at the head of the bay. And he will call his girlfriend, and plead with her to just talk to him please just talk to him.

At home, my feet out of their work-shoes will be swollen and bear the imprint of my socks, so I put them up on the coffee table and decide to skip laundry. I think about the girl from Tuamotu with her anklet of pearl, and try to name her — Afaitu? Poe? — but in ten thousand years there are more names than even I can remember.

◆

Though it began last night when Charlie felt the wave close over his head, that — like the Walkman, like the button — was only the harbinger. One of the youngest ones, just twenty, assigned to the meticulous work of the teaspoon and the whisk, finds a Starbucks mug showing the name and skyline of an unfamiliar city.

"I don't know," she says. For a moment she is stupid. She thinks the mistake is hers, and she'll get in trouble for digging into the wrong past. She looks through the earth to comfort herself with familiar things, the threads of a cedar apron, the abalone spangles. Instead she uncovers a flip phone with a pink sparkly butterfly sticker on the back. It's covered in ash. If they had a Geiger counter it would tick.

"What did you *do?*" Charlie asks the girl when she shows him the flip phone. He didn't sleep well last night, and when he did sleep he dreamed of deep water. His forehead muddy where he scratched in the compulsive motion he makes when he is anxious, and his work goes poorly. When he's not working, he thinks — incessantly — about the moment of submersion.

Though he snaps at them, it doesn't stop. They find PDAs and Tamagotchis, a bottle of Spelman's Elixir ca. 1873. A single white tennis sock with a pale pink bobble folded as though to protect the delicate whale-bone hook from an antique carver of great art. Find greenstone from Aotearoa, and black argillite that traveled down the coast from the Gwaii in the foot of a canoe. Find a bladder of oolichan oil. Find Oribeware, up the coast from what is just now called "Oregon," the result of a shipwrecked Japanese fishing boat in an earlier millennium. Find a single page of that *Rolling Stone* from 1993, with Janet Jackson on the cover.

Charlie sweats through his khaki camp shirt. He stops the three who've uncovered the *Rolling Stone* and calls them all to the tent. It is summer again, after the previous day's unseasonable rain. They think he's going to reveal something to him, some plan, some theory.

"That's it for today," is all Charlie says, after a long moment in which he stares at their assembled feet. "Go on back to the house."

When they troop past, I see the beer-enthusiast text his silent girlfriend, thumbs jabbing his unnameable anxiety onto the screen, though he deletes the words before he can send them.

Charlie, left behind, stops his work to stare out into the bay. Despite my little gift of the previous night, he is too stupid to know that he stands on time's fault line. The kids know better than to play there, and the teenagers don't go there at night to drink and fuck in secret, though it's far enough from town to be suitable for both activities.

But Charlie is not clever, so he keeps digging, alone, and finds a piece of gorilla glass and aluminum fused in an unfamiliar configuration, embedded deep in what must have been hot ash. A tetrapack of juice with a chip that raves in a thin, repetitive voice about the miraculous properties of its organic Jaboncilla.

It is not the noisy tetrapack, nor the evidence of ash that surrounds the unfamiliar hardware that stops him. It is the skull just visible beneath the most ancient layer at the bottom of the pit. A skull that — when it is disinterred — bears the irrefutable signs of an embedded electronic device, gold fused to the bone at the right temple beside a worn hole — trepanning of a still-to-come kind — where filaments once passed into the long-gone brain.

When he reaches the skull Charlie leaves without saying anything, and walks up to the restaurant, which is empty but for me at a table where I can watch the door, wrapping flatware in paper napkins.

"Charlie," I say, as he pushes the plastic ribbons aside and comes in. "Charlie?"

"Oh," he says. "Right, it's …?"

"Lin."

"Okay, Lynn," he says. "Can I get some coffee." It looks like a question, but it doesn't sound like one.

I gather the cup and the coffee, and I think, *it's not easy to touch the other shore.* He has been narrow-minded. He has ignored the evidence of time's instability, though it is before his eyes. But it is not easy.

"Maybe I can help," I say as I set out his coffee. "Maybe I can give you a hand."

I wait. An opportunity for repentance, I think. A chance to ask.

"Lynn, look, I'm kind of working here. I kind of need you to leave me alone."

You are insistent in your ignorance. I would like a little awe.

Lean hard. It's all there: earthquake, tsunami, subduction, meltwaters, gyres, currents, rising tides, reactors. There were prophetic dreams, and floods. Immigrants and refugees. Sasquatch and contrails and fallout shelters.

He's sweating now. He puts a hand up to his head where he sees sparks that swim — like sperm, like schools of bright-bellied fish — through his peripheral vision.

Under the silt, and hidden by the barnacles of an earlier tide-line, the bronze cannon of a Spanish galleon. There was a giantess with a basket made of snakes, kidnapping children to eat for her supper. There were gold ingots in the woods, and a set of steps carved in the granite mountainside, descending to a corridor that, once found and left, is never found again. The epoch of the glacier and the epoch of its withdrawal, when breakneck meltwaters trip down the hillsides, and all the things taken up by its dragging underbelly are revealed again to the air. I remember when we found frozen mammoths in the till of withdrawing glaciers, how we'd search them out, and relish them for the tang of extinction.

Charlie makes a sound like gurgling.

Drones. Oil spills. The ticktick of the geigercounter. The goo of dormant nanobots. Charlie's breath bubbles in his chest. Thunderbirds — a family of them lived as humans, far to the northwest of here. And, Charlie, there will be thunderbirds again. The sea withdraws or advances daily, seasonally, on an epochal clock.

The other shore is indefinite: saltwater, and fresh, stone and liquid, invertebrate and mammal, spit and inlet, then and now shoved against one another by time's tectonics. If you were a wiser man, Charlie, water logic would not so disturb you. But you are stupid, and you are small.

◆

I have often forgotten how fragile they are, thinly-armored like spot prawns, their minds translucent like the grey-green shell they call *Pododesmus macrochisma*. The high tide line I make on the inside of his skull swells one side of his face, one eye rolls up, as though he is searching the ceiling.

I am always so sorry, and it is always too late. I should be punished for what I've done, but who can punish me? There's only exile, which I chose after Afaitu, with the Tahitian pearl on her ankle, or the silly boy who lost the bone hook I carved for him with great and original art.

As I have done before, I should walk into the island's interior valleys, and live with the mountain lion and the argumentative *corvidae*. I should walk until I can no longer hear the sea, and then walk further, and wait for the terminal wave that is, one day, coming, soon, yesterday, tomorrow, that will disorder time with its passage, or has already done so, that will leave nothing in its wake. Not even me.

Story Notes

I've lived far from the Salish Sea for a long time now, but my mind and heart still live there, a connection that's acutely painful in crisis. When you live near the Cascadia Subduction Zone, you're always waiting for "The Big One," the megathrust earthquake that's going to happen sometime between this afternoon and five hundred years from now. Dread is written deeply into your heart when you're a kid doing earthquake drills at school, or lying in your bed at night and rehearsing your escape, planning which doorway or interior wall you'll hide against if you feel a tremor.

"Thank You For Your Patience" is also about the painful combination of intimacy and distance we experience when our loved ones are spread across the world. You have the god's-eye-view of the satellite, or the Google search that lets you follow in excruciating detail fire or flood on the other side of the world. It's hard to look away when witness seems to be the only action available to you. That was how I experienced COVID–19, the strange tension between the quiet streets around our house and the chaos in other cities and families. We know so much about a world we can't see, and care about people who appear to us only as digital words in a text message, or electronic voices. But even if we are far away, our response is visceral, because those tenuous, transcontinental connections are real, and planted firmly in our hearts.

Thank You For Your Patience

I'm lucky because they replaced a bunch of chairs last month and I got a new one. A good chair is important when you spent ten hours a day in a cubicle talking to strangers about their problems. I've been here three years and worked on most of Westermorgen's services which means I can with no thought help grandma set up her Wi-Fi. Or troubleshoot banking software. Or set up your cellphone plan or help you with some app designed to find your soulmate that nevertheless fills you with hopelessness.

(I can't help you with the hopelessness.)

It's nonstandard, but I'm Westermorgen's floater, and Geordie or Keersty drop me where the calls are heavy or turnover is high. I can answer questions within five seconds of some asshole in Toronto posting wtf my TV doesn't see the house network. And I respond, *I'm sorry to hear that @TOasshole let's see if I can help.* I'm impossible to rile because I've heard everything, every possible stupid question, every strange request regarding lapsed policies and missed payments, every paranoid rant, every sort of impotent rage. The management is shitty and the customers are irritable, but there's beauty in problem solving.

The really bad stuff started at the end of last month, when I had to do a 1on1 with Geordie, teamlead for the floor. I'd been fielding a bunch of questions regarding a recent patch that had broken everything. I had this rhythm hitting my 30s AHT and typing without thinking, *Mark here how can I help you*. But 1on1 is a mandated interruption, so I listened to Geordie brainstorm about improving morale. They stopped having barbecues because it was too expensive even when the burgers were sawdust and soy. Also no one wanted to be outside because Detroit was still burning and the ppm up to something like LA in fire season.

"Listen to this. Westermorgen Idol," Geordie told me. "We judge three of the top ranked calls and we have a thing and some-one walks away with a Timmy's gift card. Like, fifty bucks."

Geordie said that like it was a good thing.

"What about a key fob?" I asked. We can't get out without one after hours, but only management can hold. "Or the winner gets to wear jeans. Or keep their phone for a shift?" That didn't rate an answer. The most frustrating thing about Westermorgen is that teamleads have to hold your phone, like you're an untrust-worthy teenager who's been grounded. I feel like I'm lost in a cave or a space station. When I do a lot of overtime I arrive when it's dark and I leave when it's dark and while sometimes I go around the corner for coffee or McNuggets, it always feels like I'm just visiting the world. I don't know what's happened: if a government's fallen, or an ice shelf has collapsed, if Detroit is burning again, or maybe California, or the Great Lakes are dying at a slightly faster rate than they were when I left for work.

Never knowing what's going on outside, I sit in my good chair and say, *That sounds frustrating*, to everyone, no matter who's talk-ing or what they want. *Let me see if I understand your problem*.

"You could judge," Geordie said, still talking about morale. "You're impartial. You hate everyone."

"I don't hate everyone, Geordie," I said reflexively, though to be fair, I hate a lot of people here.

After my mandated fifteen minutes with Geordie, I saw that Misty had a problem with my documentation, which has been rough since they changed policy on me. She's in the Philippines where most of the real work happens. Upper management is all in India. They only have us because they need Canadian accents on the phones, and they get tax breaks, bringing jobs to one of the more desolate parts of the country. Downwind from Detroit, rampant West Nile, and ninety percent of the province's heavy metals processed at the plant out by the mall. Seventy percent of the babies born here are girls, something to do with residual BPA.

Misty is on the other side of the Pacific, in Legazpi, but you'd think she was right here, considering how aggressively she organizes us.

ur shit at filling the forms mark the write up is going to kill ur rank

We're stack ranked every shift. It gets you points you can redeem which, honestly, is worth it for the grocery store gift cards.

Just tell me what I did wrong, Legazpi.

✦

We were in the middle of a rough month. The flu hit everywhere at once and no one could afford to lose the work, so we had a bunch of people come in sick, coughs and juicy sneezes all over the floor, and half the time you got on the elevator and everyone was grey-faced and weaving.

I came in over the weekend to cover mobile because they lost half their staff, so I'd been on for eight days by Monday when Geordie was manic trying to call people in so he won't have to go on phones. He always says, when we're smoking outside and he's pointedly not looking at the place where the GM building used to be, *it's not the extra fifty cents an hour, it's the fact that I don't have to deal with people.* He hated taking calls.

He offered me overtime, so I started coming in at six and leaving at ten, and I didn't even notice the weekend. I do remember going home those nights and thinking how hollow my room felt, with my roommates playing CoD in the living room, and how my body seemed to vibrate. Caffeine maybe, or pseudoephedrine. I heard phantom time warnings and chimes, and when I closed my eyes I could see the screen and call after call flooding the queue. By Saturday, Westermorgen was a haunted house, but I still wasn't sick.

That sounds frustrating. Let me see if I can help.

I was dealing with this woman on Vancouver Island who couldn't generate invoices. We'd been at it for two hours and I could feel her getting upset when I told her to wipe the whole system and start again. I can help you do that, but she was like, *no we'll lose two weeks of work*, and there's nothing I can say to that, so we keep troubleshooting even though it's pointless.

"Okay, I said, can you go back to the root invoice and try —"

"— oh," she said, "is that —"

And that was it, I didn't hear anything but the line itself, which just went dead, that kind of absence you get when someone hangs up on you.

"Are you there? Ma'am?"

I called back but I got a re-order tone — not voicemail, or an old-fashioned busy signal, but the one that means the whole system is busy or blocked or down.

I dropped out of the queue then, which you're not supposed to do obviously, and went looking for Geordie, who was chatting with Keersty about Westermorgen Idol. I asked if they knew anything but of course they didn't and when I asked if I could at least grab my phone to see what was happening, Keersty did a kind of elementary-school-teacher sigh.

documentation for #3990180 ur overdue mark.

Caller dropped

saw that. explanation?

Happening across the board. Looks like the problem is at their end.

I didn't find out until Mo came back from break streaked wet in the way you are if you've run out into that rain blowing in from Detroit because you don't want it to touch your skin, saying, "Earthquake on the west coast. You know anyone out there?" I think about the woman trying to get the invoice together for a tiny order of sea salt from some equally tiny place on Vancouver Island, her business so minuscule it all fit into our cheapest sub-scription. In my unsubmitted documentation for Misty I had written that her voice sounded like a hopeful, but-slightly-overwhelmed Great Aunt trying to make the remote control work.

"No one. How bad?"

"Like 9.6. The worst since forever. For hundreds of years."

"Jesus," I said, "Jesus. Jesus."

✦

I've had similar moments on calls. When the shooting happened in Montreal — not vieux Montreal, but the one where the kids ran downtown away from McGill, and the photographer caught the girl as the bullet tore out her right kneecap — I was on the line with this dickwad in a coworking space on Maisonneuve who was asking to talk to my supervisor. Then — mid whine — he stopped talking, like he suddenly didn't care about my attitude. I could hear his phone pinging.

"Sir, are you there?"

"Can you hear that? It's happening on the street. I can see —"

A faint popping. Voices raised and doors slammed. Then he cut the call.

I kept in the queue. I helped someone update. I did a sub-scription renewal. The next person, though, needed a backup and that took forever so we chatted about hockey until she said, "Did you hear about Montreal?"

"No ma'am," I said, thinking about that sound I maybe heard before his phone cut. Firecrackers. Backfires.

"Some guys shot up the whole downtown. I think it was terrorists. Who knows. FLQ? Or Muslims maybe. Red Power. Fifty dead but it was going up every time I refreshed the page."

She kept going on like this while we did a backup and then I made sure everything worked and it had been like three hours at that point, and I kept thinking of the guy and his silence, and what was going on in the streets while we talked about his login and how unprofessional I was. I don't have any friends in Montreal. I went there once to drink when I was eighteen, but that's it. I just had that guy and the thump of footsteps fleeing the co-working space.

When I took my break the rain was falling again, the faintly grey kind that runs down the sidewalks and the gutters and when it builds up enough you can see that it's a little milky because it's full of ash. If you think too hard about what's running into your eyes as you stand outside, smoking until your pack is empty, you go eat a twenty-four box of Timbits, or six Big Macs, or you stop for one beer on the way home and only leave when they push you out the door.

Geordie was outside. I gave him a cigarette even though he doesn't smoke either, and he said, "it doesn't seem to be getting cleaner. Wasn't it supposed to get cleaner?" He grew up in Detroit, though he was already over here when it burned last year.

"Maybe it's safer. The hum is worse. I thought the hum was supposed to go when they sent in the clean up crews."

We watched the warm, ash-colored water run down the gutters until it was ankle deep. The city is a wetland, and there isn't far for water to go, so it ends up in people's basements, all that ashy, bony water running through foundations and drains, a constant trickle in the background. Sort of like the faint pop you might hear while you're on the phone with a guy in Montreal who wants to talk to your manager.

"Does it feel —" Geordie says and lights another cigarette.

"What, Geordie?" I hate how often he doesn't finish his sentences.

"Does it feel like it's happening more often? This kind of thing?"

I drop my smoke into the rainwater and shrug, then say, "I wish I knew what to tell you." Which wasn't a real answer, and I used my tech support voice when I said it because I didn't want to have that conversation.

✦

On my first break after the earthquake, I smoked and watched the rain and videos on my phone, someone livestreaming the moment it hit — boring talk about food or weather, then a strange look on their face, their eyes dart upward, then the phone falls. Overhead footage from helicopters of downtown Vancouver, all those green towers swaying and falling, and the bridge swinging until the cables snap like rubber bands. The worst in recorded history. Worse, probably, than the last megathrust in 1700. I just kept thinking of that woman, and the sort of quiet shock in her voice, her "oh — is that —" and then nothing, and I was standing out in the rain, but still warm, when it occurred to me that I might have heard her last words. I kept thinking about the texture of the silence after the call dropped and what had happened the moment after that, if that had been the worst of it, the shock of the whole world rumbling.

Or if it had been worse for her after that, or right now, or tomorrow.

I only had ten minutes because call volume was increasing. My throat was starting to tickle, and the world — just suddenly, out of nowhere — started to look glassy, the light thick from the ceiling squares, and my skin prickled when I ran my hands over my arms, which were covered with goose bumps.

The floor was nearly empty except for Geordie running around supervising and not taking calls, and the queue was packed. My first call was from way north along the coast, Prince Rupert, a woman calling about a password reset. "I want Mark," she said. "He helped me before. Can I talk to Mark?"

While I was documenting I thought, fuck it, I'm going to tell Misty what the woman told me while we were waiting for the password reset email, about how when you're that far north you don't notice time passing, and you feel good in an unimaginable way in summer, luminous and hopeful, and how in winter all you want to do is die and drink yourself into a coma, so you know, it balances out.

After that I reopened #3990180.

An elderly woman, I wrote, *on a phone, trying to print invoices for locally produced sea salt, looks over at the rack of glass jars in which she keeps her stock because she hears a rattle, then another, then she says, "oh — is that —" and nothing else because at that moment, the force of twenty-five thousand Hiroshimas lit the Cascadia Subduction Zone — on which Vancouver island rests like a cork on a bottle — centuries of continental tension released.*

I type that, then I hit send, then I add a secondary note on her file. *At 8.32 PST a 9.8 hit the Cascadia Subduction Zone.*

And Misty was right there on ChatHive, not telling me it was Inappropriate. She wrote, *rest their souls*, and I was comforted by those temporary words, which surprised me.

my grandparents were on mindanao in the 1976 earthquake. u got anyone there?

No

I heard the hum from Detroit. It was, somehow, a relief to know that across the world Misty was in a similar room among people evaluating documentation for apps and ISPs and account-ing software. People saying, *that must be frustrating, let's see if I can help*. Something occurred to me.

You hear anything about tsunamis?

no word so far

Do you have your phone? So you can get the alerts?

theyll let us know. we're so bad im taking calls so i won't be fixing ur doc until tomorrow

I wondered if Keersty would let us know, or if she would dither about it until all we could do was climb to the top floor of the building and watch a wave consume what was left of Detroit before it swamped us, too.

Five more calls and I refilled my water bottle — the one with the slogan on it, *fueling small business with the tools to succeed*, that some now-lost Westermorgen contract brought in — and I was looking at my skin reflected in the sink, which was the color of those pale, lumpy smokers you see outside the entrance, the color of an uncooked chicken nugget. I felt adrenalized, like a moment before I'd been terrified, but I could not remember how or why. I wondered what it was doing to me, inside, all those cells now remade into virus factories, turning to goo and mush and slough-ing off while the virus proliferated through my system, and I left traces on everything I touched.

The water ran over the top of the bottle. Clear. So far the ash hasn't worked its way through the city's water system. Or maybe it had and it was invisible like the microplastics in the lake.

"So, you going to judge?" It was Geordie. "We're going to do it next week. I was thinking we'd set a time limit. Like, five minute calls. You and me and Keersty judge it. I grabbed fifty for the Timmy's card, too."

"Man," I said, "man."

Geordie just stared at me. "You getting sick? You know what you need to do is ..." He went on about Echinacea or FluFX and I thought about the tsunami that was, or was not, traveling across the Pacific. "... Or just hammer your system with anti-oxidants, and take a double dose of Nyquil —"

Without thinking I pulled my phone out of my pocket.

"— You know you can't have that anywhere near the floor."

I was already googling "Pacific tsunami alert," and it was rolling rainbows and I stared at it so hard that it seemed to take over the whole world, and then I shivered, but Geordie was still talking.

"Don't make me write you up. I don't want to deal with it."

"K," I said.

"It's about privacy for our users. They need to know they can trust our integrity, our word, and our system."

The poster on the far side of the break room said "Integrity," "Word," and "System." I saw that the alert had been issued for Japan. That's when he took my phone.

"You fuck the dog, I have to write you up. I don't want to write you up."

Japan in six hours. Eight pm. I'd still be here, while very far away a wave crested on the seacoast, filling the river basins and the car parks.

✦

I know you don't have to surrender your phone, even if they can require you to leave it at home. I know they're not supposed to lock you in, either, or let you smoke within three meters of the door, even when the ash is falling. They're not supposed to pay you in points you can then exchange for grocery store gift cards, which you need because the new minimum wage doesn't even cover rent. But I need a job.

The next call I got was farther south, closer to the epicenter. The first thing I did was ask about the earthquake.

"We felt it, and there's the tsunami warning, but we're far enough inland it shouldn't be —"

"— Tsunami warning?"

"So when I try to log in —"

— Tsunami?

"— I keep getting the same error, it says my account's frozen. What does that mean? I need to do some invoices. And yeah, I just got the text like half an hour ago. Landfall is like an hour."

The account was frozen due to missed payments, so I pointed that out and the guy insisted no he'd set up an automated transfer and he kept me on the line while he chatted with the bank's tech support on another line to sort out the direct deposit, and then I reactivated his account, all this time the tsunami traveling toward the coast, where the shallower bottom would raise the wave's height by narrowing its length because the last time I'd been outside I'd looked at a gif on Wikipedia that demonstrated how Tsunamis crest as they travel through shallow waters.

The last thing he said wasn't *thanks*, it was, "There it is, the tide's going way out, I hope everyone's out of downtown." Then he was gone, and I could imagine it, the water running away from shore, like a huge exhalation, and then collecting into a rising wave that will destroy them all.

The tsunami warning? I wrote in ChatHive, hoping Misty was there.

Keersty responded instantly: *That is not appropriate ChatHive is for important work stuff.*

we havent heatd anything but were swamped so who knows what going on outside

CHATHIVE CHANNEL WILL ONLY BE USED FOR APPRORPAITE BUSINESS RELATED BUSINESS.

Maybe you should get out anyway.

CHATHIVE CHANNEL WILL ONLY BE USED FOR APPRORPAITE BUSINESS RELATED BUSINESS.

CHATHIVE CHANNEL WILL ONLY BE USED FOR APPRORPAITE BUSINESS RELATED BUSINESS.

✦

I'd been there for sixteen hours, and I couldn't remember the last time I slept a full night at home, when I hadn't been buzzed on cold pills and exhaustion, and the sound of CoD from the living room. That week when I did sleep I kept saying, *This is Mark from Magnacorp* or *This is Mark from Wherever I Am Right Now,* and heard explosions and the way voices carry over the river from Detroit, the screams and the crowds and the gunshots. Or maybe I was never actually asleep, maybe I was just off my head. I shouldn't have washed the pills down with beer, but there's that thing that happens when you stop in for a beer after work and the inertia of the whole thing, the job, the shitty beer and the fact that a person brings you food, even if you can't afford it, that sticks you to your seat. It was bad last summer when we couldn't afford to run the AC but the bar on the way home could, and it was full of familiar guys, broke and lonely and trying to avoid looking at what was left of the Detroit skyline, or the grey-green clouds boiling to the north, and the hail and the lightning storms every afternoon like clockwork. The summers are definitely hotter, and the mosquitoes are definitely worse, and last summer I noticed that the birds don't sing anymore, all their whistles sound like videogame lasers.

I stepped outside for a cigarette and realized the doors had been locked and I don't have a fob because I don't rate a fob. Geordie was there too, setting up his stupid Westermorgen Idol, piles of bright pink and green and blue postit notes all over his desk.

"I need to go out."

"The doors are locked for the night."

"I need to get out."

"We lost another girl from Online. You'll have to take over social media if we lose anyone else. Take your break here."

I just kind of stared at him and my skin prickled like all the pseudoephedrine I'd taken had rushed to the surface and was blasting every single nerve ending in my body.

"I need to go outside."

"You *can't*. Like, you physically can't."

I kind of stood there and I'm ashamed to say I wanted to cry. Like a little kid who isn't allowed to use the bathroom, or who just wants to sit with his Dad but keeps getting dragged away by un-familiar relatives. The kind of crying you see on the bus at rush hour when some little kid coming back from the mall loses it and lies in the aisle wailing, cramming road salt in his mouth, and you think *you and me both*.

I didn't actually cry. I hate myself, because I just said, begging, "Can I please can I have my phone back, please?"

Geordie looked at me like I was an idiot, him in the middle of all the post-it notes that read CONGRATULATIONS! or YOUR A WINNER! or WESTERMORGEN IDOL!!!

I didn't say anything. I left. At first I sat in the lunch room, shivering and nauseous, staring at a plastic solo cup leftover from the barbecues they used to give before the ash. There will be worse moments in my life no doubt — more pain, more sadness — but I can't imagine anything so wide-ranging in its desolation as that moment. The only thing I could focus on was telling Misty to get her phone back and watch the horizon and be ready to escape.

A girl from Online staggered through, sweaty and pale, and I knew that Geordie would be here in a moment to ask for another eight hours, overnight, answering strangers' questions so perfectly that they all treat me like a shitty customer service AI built to serve.

There aren't a lot of choices in your life, are there? You can choose to have kids, or not, or leave your hometown or not. Or to stay in a terrible job you are, for some reason, very good at. But other than that, what is there? Just a lot of compliance and non-compliance. This didn't feel like a choice. I said to the girl, "We need to get out of here," and she nodded. Then we headed down to the lobby. The doors were locked and no one carrying a key was in the building and the girl looked bad, but when I went to the fire escape she still said, "No, we're not supposed to!"

"We need to get out —"

"— they'll *fire* us!" And I could hear the fear in her voice, and I wondered how badly she needed this job, that she was here in the middle of the night, so sick she could hardly stand.

"Tell them I did it," I said, and hit the bar.

Only it didn't move because it was locked, too. The next thing I did was stupid, but I don't know what else I could have done. I walked back to the lobby and picked up a garbage can and began slamming it into the glass door. Behind me she was just coughing and coughing and said, maybe, *stop stop*, but so faintly I could ignore it. Then we were out, and she was staggering toward the

Emergency room on Ouellette and I was alone in rainwater the same temperature as my blood. Then I went looking for a payphone because the only way to sort this out was to call in, but I couldn't remember which of Westermorgen's departments Misty was assigned to so when I finally found the city's last payphone — in the bus depot — I called them all, all the sad voices of men and women here and on the other side of the world.

"Welcome to Caiphas Business Systems, Jane speaking, how can I help you?" "Welcome to Tesla Mobility, how can I help you?" "Welcome to Roscommon Account Services." "Welcome to Light-house Mobility."

"I'm looking for Misty. She helped me before."

"I'm sure I can help you. What's your user number?"

"Misty. Misty knows," I said, my voice querulous and elderly. "Put on Misty!"

I could hear the exhaustion in his silence, then the compli-ance. "One moment, and I'll transfer you."

"Hey, Misty." I said, "Misty. Misty. You need to get to high ground."

"What? Who is this?"

"Just promise, k?"

"There's no tsunami warning —"

"— it's on its way. It's passing Japan and Hawaii. It hit the Aleutians. California." I hoped she didn't mistake me for what I felt like, right then: a crazy old man, mad with loneliness, longing to hear a voice in the void, even if it was only to harangue them for the weakness of their service and the terrible nature of their product.

"Mark?"

"Another six hours to landfall. I know you'll still be on shift. Promise."

I waited for her to disconnect, which was okay because at least I'd told her. Then I think maybe she said, "Thank you, Mark," or maybe it was just the noise in my head. I held the line another moment, then hung up. I felt okay because I'd got through, because I wasn't in a cubicle anymore, because I could walk home and enjoy the silence before CoD marathons in the living room, enjoy the ashy rain falling across my slowly cooking skin.

I walked home hoping Misty said, "Thank you, Mark." It felt like I was slipping through a gap in the world, between noises, a kind of silent passage, the way kids slip along the abandoned rail easements in town, below grade, the corridors of grass and rats and squirrels and birds. Between the noise of the phones and CoD. Between heartbeats. Between cresting waves, the silence you hang onto for just a moment when someone hangs up, before you go onto the next call because there is, temporarily, a respite from the tyranny of the queue. The silence after a bullet connects, or a wave hits on the other side of the world. I just hoped, harder and harder and harder, that Misty would insist they unlock the doors and break the windows and they could escape before the wave arrived to wash the rest of us away.

Story Notes

This is a story about how the world ends for one woman on an island in the Salish Sea. With that end comes the birth of another sort of world, a terrifying but necessary adaptation to the changes of the Anthropocene. The story is also about the transfiguration of flesh into newer and stranger forms — a kind of material afterlife. While the story is horror, I guess, I find it quite hopeful. We have borrowed the substance in our bodies from algae and stardust and oceans, and when that material leaves our form, it might still bear our stamp, the way the colonies that form around a whale fall bear the outline of the whale. Even when we're alive, we exist in collaboration with other organisms, a collection that briefly calls itself "I." The bletted Woman's afterlife continues in much the same way, with an even more complex collaboration, and a resurrection of the compost heap rather than the soul.

The Bletted Woman

When a medlar is ripe it is hard and mouth-puckering, but a few weeks after it falls, cell walls rupture and enzymes convert starches to sugars — a process known as *bletting*. Incipient decay renders the medlar's flesh fragrant, like caramel and rose hip. Judith told Ben (though he didn't listen that time because he'd heard it all before) that every bletted medlar is a reminder of what the world used to taste like, when our milk ripened to yogurt in the dairy, and we seeded pecorino with *Piophila casei* maggots to make casu marzu. There is, she lectured, a whole catalogue of flavors eliminated if you insist on the preservation of flesh in its first or even second youth.

"Rot is not a failure," she told Ben when he saw her eating the first medlar she picked and bletted. It was November, and the world had not yet ended. "Rot is a transitional state of matter."

Normally he would accuse her of Judith-splaining, since he already knew her theories on the material afterlives of flesh, but this time he was so horrified by what she was eating, he only said, "Jude, are you serious? It looks like —"

"— I know what it looks like. I really don't need you to say—"

"— It looks like —"

"— I know!"

She dug her spoon between the pips, squeezing the thin, papery-wet skin — loose with age — so the last brown flesh oozed out. Slack like honeyed apple sauce, but with the fragrance of a golden plum.

"Delicious," she mumbled and licked a brown smudge from her finger.

So it is with our bodies in their long afterlives.

♦

Judith's mother was sixty-two when she died, six years after a diagnosis of early onset dementia, so Judith had already guessed what caused her new disorientation, her emotional liability and frustration and forgetfulness, the failures of taste and smell that made the medlar bitter. At first these had just seemed the new order of widowhood in the wake of Ben's death. Having learned a lot from her mother's decline, she was already well organized. She had an elaborate note system that synced across all platforms automatically, and she installed a shelf by her front door on which she instantly placed her keys, wallet, and phone, so that even on days of strangulating disorientation, her body might still remember the location of her keys.

Judith settled on the medlar as her emblem in the last waiting room of her diagnosis (which smelled not of death, but of some leafy fragrance in a diffuser). The doctor confirmed what an earlier DNA test had already suggested. He talked about managing symptoms. He talked about her team. A social worker. A neurologist. Medications. Therapies.

"Okay," Judith said limply. They sat for a long, quiet moment. A computer chirruped.

"Is there anything you want to ask?"

"There isn't a cure."

"Not yet." He paused, like he expected something more, then, "Are you here alone? Can we call someone? You probably shouldn't drive."

Judith nodded. Waited an appropriate amount of time. Drove herself home, enjoying the sensation of choice while she still had it.

At work she wrote a training manual. She sat on the hiring committee for her replacement. On October first, she carried medlars in from the back garden, taking care not to overload her back. Then she wondered if her back was something she should bother guarding. She looked up at the translucent blue sky, and for a moment allowed herself to stop the busily resistant schedule she had established for herself. This schedule existed mostly to protect others from her own impending death, to shore up her living will, and to ensure that at particular milestones she would be removed from her job, her car, her stove, her home. She would not plow through a summer festival on a closed street. She would not set off an explosion with an unattended stove. She would not be pried out of her house like a living corpse, throwing grocery bags full of shit at the public health officers.

Then one evening she came home to a message from a soft-voiced woman representing The Institute for Advanced Study. There were possibilities. She had been recommended. For the first time since before Ben she felt something like hope. In another leaf-scented room, she sat with a folder open across her lap, in it a list of questions regarding her diagnosis and her mental suitability to undertake an experimental procedure that would allow her to experience the afterlife of the flesh. The right responses to the survey seemed obvious: she answered dishonestly that she had never considered suicide, honestly that she had often — since her diagnosis — thought about her death.

She was nothing if not reasonable, and the list she made only expanded as she decided to take up The Institute's offer for a useful death: Fill out the form. No suicide. Much death. Make a second genetic profile to see if I am suitable for the procedure. Sign an NDA. Do the interviews and follow the course they have set out. A bacteriophage. A new and toxic strain of Streptococci. Certain genetically altered flukes. An invitation to local strains of yeast and mold. Pentobarbitol. An ending.

✦

Of course, the world started ending long before Ben died, and before her diagnosis, and before the bletted flesh of the medlar grew bitter on her tongue. The November of her diagnosis she scooped it into her mouth and tasted nothing, no rose hip plum, no dream-apple, only the incipient slime of decay on her palate, fuzzing her mouth like blood. One more disappointment caused by neurological changes associated with early onset dementia. Or by changes in the microbial processes that had once rendered the flesh sweet. She wasn't sure which it was.

The end of the human world began with the systematic destruction of human microbiomes, eradicated by refined sugar and hand sanitizer, sparkling kitchen counters and too-clean fingernails and children who never played outside because the cities were grey with 600ppm. The remaining human microbiome continued its evolution, with once-friendly species dying off, so the guts of the global north turned to a monoculture, then a desert, and we were abandoned to our isolated, disinfected little worlds, as sugary as the garbage bins behind an old fashioned ice cream shop. While there had been inklings of the possible consequences of this microbial die-off, we were unprepared for just how far-reaching the effects would be: Alzheimer's, diabetes, obesity, schizophrenia, IBS, any number of other mood disorders. And that was just the absence of friendly microorganisms. There was also the slow spread of stranger species, toxic to the human body, new descendants of *C. botulinum* (unsuitable for cosmetic procedures, that killed you within four hours of contamination), chlorine-loving MRSA shut down the public swimming pools, and cyanobacteria bloomed in warm groundwater, the earth's microbiota evolving rapidly in directions increasingly toxic to humans.

Judith had done her part to preserve microscopic life, with a kitchen full of fermenting mason jars, filling the house with the fecal stench of rotten cabbage. She had made kimchi, and sauerkraut, and kombucha. Her charcuterie, her beer, her bread, her yogurt, all vivid with the tang of organisms invisible, except in the blue-green stains they left on cambozola and the dusty casing of salami. She had raised and destroyed whole microscopic empires at the back of her fridge and cultivated vital microbiomes even in the middle of the grey-skyed and toxic city where all the earthworms in their garden died, and only poisonous extremophile superbugs and tardigrades could survive. She cultivated bacterial mats deep inside, too, on her skin, her eyes, her mouth, her vagina, her cuts. She rejected bleach. She dug in the dirt with bare hands and walked barefoot until she was host to a benign colony of hookworms. Until the bees died, she ate hyperlocal urban honey. She celebrated her microbial *terroir*, contaminants gathered in a lifetime of travel and ferment. Not that it did her any good, as her brain turned to plaque and she forgot Ben's name sometimes, and when she did remember — on those temporary clear days, when the coffee shop once again made sense and she knew what to buy at the grocery store — she remembered when her mother forgot the word "Judith" and how it had broken her heart.

◆

The Institute owned a small, chilly island in the north Pacific, more than eight hours' travel from Judith's house. When she locked the door that morning she thought, *goodbye goodbye forever*, then she embarked on the first of four flights. The second-to-last flight landed in a tiny regional airport, where she arrived sweaty and disoriented, glad to be collected by a friendly stranger whose face seemed familiar. If she had been alone, she would have wept and shouted and given up then, fixing herself to the parking lot and surrendering to her disintegrating brain. But the man shook her hand and held it, and said his name was Sadik, curly grey hair, but a young face, and one of those gentle smiles that seemed to encourage confession. They were delayed, he said, by weather in from the Pacific, a sweetly scented chinook, which used to be unseasonable before the climate began its change. Then there was a long, awful moment when Judith could not be sure where she was, and her eyes again turned north, and she thought, *this must be the end of the world.*

"Do you know," Sadik said brightly, like a travel brochure, and she was glad he didn't seem to notice her confusion, "our island was originally a burial ground?"

"Oh," she said through the noise in her head, and then tried to think of something else to say. "Oh."

Thankfully, he went on. "It's a humane and sensible way to dispose of our bodies. Very clean. Supports local scavengers. The council preserved the sites in collaboration with our organization. The monuments are quite moving. We can visit them if you like."

"Oh."

"Do you believe in an afterlife?" the man asked abruptly.

"I must," she said. "I'm here, aren't I?"

She would have said more if she could, but the only thing that came to mind would be too hard to explain, since the rational argument had disintegrated and left only potent and tangled images in her heart. A medlar. A whale fall. A nurse-log. The dead laid out for sun and scavengers to transfigure. Their souls — whatever that meant — having fled, but the order they left behind remains in those disintegrating bodies. Whales are still, she thought, the presiding form, decades after their fall. You can see the nurse-log's outline in the growth patterns of the trees it once supported. Human beings, she thought, might leave a similar imprint on the world when they pass from it, but it was too hard to explain without talking about medlars. And it was too hard to think of her medlar tree, and how its fruit would fall, ungathered, bletting for the ants, if any ants survived in her garden.

"But you know," she managed to say in the silence they shared, staring into the grey fog wall. Her eyes strained to focus on that nothing. "We're all something's afterlife, right? Because everything that we're made out of was once something else. And I don't remember what it was like to be a turtle, or the left leg of a chicken, or the earthworms that ate the soil that fed the grass that fed the cattle that fed my Mom that glass of milk she drank when she was pregnant. But it's all there. Carbon and hydrogen and oxygen. So there's definitely an afterlife. It's just not personal."

"What if it could be?" Sadik asked.

She couldn't answer that. The whale fall and the medlars and Ben jumbled in her head until all she could see was rye splashing from her glass and over the gunwale, when the wind picked up and the wave-slap grew louder and faster and they had to turn around, her hands were so cold, she couldn't grip the glass, so she let it go too and return to the sand that was its previous form, somewhere near his already sea-changing body. *These are pearls that were his eyes.* A memory so vital, could her mind really be failing?

"Are you a chaplain?" she asked.

"No."

"Or," she said. "Or. Or. An exorcist?"

He laughed. "No. We don't need exorcists."

The weather broke late that afternoon, sunlight — daffodil yellow — in from the west, under the lifting storm. One minute she was staring at a blank cloud wall, then it thinned and she saw through it to an island. A dark-green smudge on the horizon. "There," Sadik said. "That's it. That's the island."

The last island, she thought, and welcomed it. Sort of.

◆

The island was rocky, covered in low Sitka spruce blown permanently eastward by the wind off the Pacific. The facility was set back from the shore, and they approached it along a cedar boardwalk up from the dock where the floatplane taxied in. Ahead of them, a woman in a white uniform carried two coolers marked with red crosses, sprinting to the low-set complex built into the granite.

"Do they worry about sea levels?"

"No."

That stopped her. "Is this. This. Thing. Supposed to fix it?"

It smelled like rain, which reminded Judith of something sad she couldn't name. Her heart beat wonky and she tried to find the lost thing. Something. Something about leaves in a garden and rain.

"Nothing's going to fix *that*. But if we know more, maybe we'll have a chance in whatever the world is about to become." He stepped past her, and she found she had been standing still a long time, so then she followed after him. At the big front doors — glass, set in a two-story atrium that was warm and rain-lashed, the glass skylights beading with fog, the cedar paneling smelling sweetly of the fire in the huge stone fireplace.

"It's out there," she said, before Sadik could lead her to the front desk where another young woman typed on a keyboard made of light. She said, pointing through the building, to a wall. "Can I go see it?"

"Yes," he said. "Tomorrow, if you want."

That night she slept well between stiff white sheets in a room facing the water, in a quiet wing far from the walled garden. She heard waves. She wondered what other candidates had slept there, who now slept elsewhere, or not at all. When she woke in the darkness she didn't know where she was, and she didn't care.

The next morning, she and Sadik sat at a refectory table made of reclaimed barn wood, their backs to the huge granite chimney and their faces to the plate glass windows.

"What brought you here?" She had enough experience with interviews to know that he had begun his examination, continuing the psychological evaluations that had begun when she applied six months before.

She was surprised to find that she had an answer already, that the question did not leave her paralyzed with doubt. She drank. She wet her lips. She said, "When Ben died he was halfway between hospitals. They'd just installed a shunt and found that he'd broken his shoulder. They didn't know when it had happened. He'd been incoherent for a week at that point, his blood pressure bottoming out again and again. He flatlined twice. I was in a car, following the ambulance. There was construction. It was raining so hard. He was dead by the time I got to Toronto Central. More or less."

Sadik waited.

"I don't want it to be like that."

"Would you like to see the garden?"

Sadik swiped a keycard and they walked through a door guarded by men in black uniforms and unobtrusive sidearms —

and then into the circular glass observation deck, punctuated by screens and sensors that recorded all activity in the corpse garden below. At first it just seemed like a large and well-tended park, but as she watched she began to see their shapes outlined in the green, which meant the more recent candidates must be out of sight, behind the granite boulders, or that tall Oregon grape. She'd seen two other candidates at lunch, but on the other side of the room, wheeled in, limbs distorted by accident or disease.

"Geonauts." Sadik said at her elbow. "That's what I call you. It hasn't caught on."

"This is where it happened?"

"Where it's happening, right now. It's not an event. It's a process."

One of the bodies in the grass moved. A faint contraction, automatic like the twitch of a dead spider's leg. A crow leapt into the air, circled, returned to the spot.

"They're still alive." It was the only way to describe what she saw.

"Not in the sense that you and I are alive. I don't think. Not after this. But the categories of 'alive' and 'dead' aren't exactly discrete here."

Another mossy human-shape shuddered.

She rested her forehead against the thick glass. Outside in the grass once-humans progressed toward their dissolution, but through The Institute's innovations, still preserved a filament of subjectivity. They were now agents on the other side of death, observing their transformation and reporting back on the experience. The hand on her shoulder was large and its fingers strong, warm through the bulky wool of her sweater. It took her a moment to realize the touch was Sadik's. It was nice to be touched. For a moment she thought of what he might look like when — but she banished the thought as frivolous.

"Ben," she said, "what if I change my mind?"

She realized what she said when the word was out of her mouth, and her heart broke, but the hand did not withdraw. She hoped he hadn't noticed.

"Would you like to sit with them?"

She nodded.

Grass had overgrown the first bodies, but she could see the limbs and hair of newer burials. No scent of rot, just the sweet decay of dead leaves in winter.

"We don't know what they're saying, but we know they're thinking." He continued easily, "our system is rudimentary, so the geonauts can tell us very little through the mycorrhizal networks. That's why we need pioneers. We need more of our kind underground, telling us what they see. Do you want to hear them?"

Sadik led her to a terminal on the observation deck. He swiped his card and tapped a screen and she heard the faint chorus of clicks and hisses.

"That's them talking?"

"Through the rhizomorphs, yes, electric pulses. Chemical signals, too. It's rudimentary, but every geonaut brings us closer to open communication with the afterlife. Or — not the afterlife, with the huge, networked biomass we belong to, but don't understand. You're listening to what we used to be. And what we go back to. What *they've* gone back to."

A click. A hiss. She held up her hand and inclined her head toward the speakers. Then Sadik offered her a pair of headphones, and she stood in the serene hallway, overlooking the corpse garden, and listened to electronic pulses from an invisible network.

"The processing is mostly done in Seattle, and we have observation sites all over the world, but this is the interface. This is where we access the network. We've known for a long time that trees communicate via their root systems and mycelia.

Rhizomorphs. And that's not even the clonal colonies of aspen, or the huge fungal networks. This is cross-species communication."

She gave up on the question she wanted to ask: was Ben out there, somewhere, despite the distance between here and there? Was he part of the same network, but so far distant his voice would be faint and tiny, translated not just by the filaments of decay — the rhizomorphs — that connected all earthly matter, but by the weight of water. The question did not form in words, and she could only feel the familiar ache of widowhood. So instead she listened to Radio Mycorrhiza. Among those noises — oh, among them somewhere — the legions of the dead might be whispering. Ben. Ben, whale-fallen Ben, speaking the pulsing language of the underworld.

The next morning, she asked Sadik if she could listen to it at night, or if one had to visit the observation deck. That afternoon he brought her a set of wireless headphones, and she heard it as soon as she put them on, a low susurration, as of leaves, a sequence of luminous gurgles and chirrups. Between meetings and blood draws from phlebotomists who rarely met her eyes, she lay in her white bed and strained her ears into the hiss of Radio Mycorrhiza. She understood nothing, but wondered if what she heard wasn't just the corpse garden and the geonauts, but other communities of microorganisms, along relays and exchanges, human or natural, chemical and electronic-pulse game of telephone, if they might reach as far as another ocean.

She wished she could ask the others how they came to this place, and what they saw when they stepped into the garden for the last time, but she knew only what Sadik knew: the susurrations and the bird-scattering twitches of the bodies under moss.

✦

Bletting only continues the material transformations called "life" during that category once called "death," more properly identified not as an event, but as a process during which the temporary patterns of conscious matter — an eye, a set of narrative memories, a brain, a point of view — are reordered into their new state, still present, but no longer in the same relation, and therefore losing the appearance of consciousness, which nevertheless may still exist if we accept consciousness as an inherent quality of matter. Ten minutes after a brain dies, delta waves can still appear on an ECG, which suggests that something called "I" might experience its own death, even before further transformations remove it from our understanding of "I."

In the case of the medlar, that new state is honeyish and fragrant.

She must have successfully converted Ben to her Gospel of Decay, because the week after his diagnosis he was researching alternative burials. He talked about carbon sequestration and rejected the incinerator at the graveyard belching him into the already filthy air. Though he rejected the cemetery, he still wanted some pageantry. He found the canvas and the cannonballs (he paid extra for Napoleonic antiques). Following his directions, Judith declined embalming and found someone who could sew him into the sheet with the cannonballs, then someone to take her and a couple of select mourners out the required minimum of three nautical miles off shore, where the water deepened. There was poetry, a ragged chorus about mist-covered mountains. They drank beer, then shots of stomach-clenching, palate-destroying rye splashed into the water as they dropped him over the side, and it was done. Out past the breakers, the islands, out in the broad Atlantic, in October, when he should have been stacking firewood on the kitchen porch, while she picked the medlars and set them in straw in the garage, to finish their transformation.

A whale fall, Ben explained to her at the end of his life, as though she didn't already know about it. Ben-splained. She listened to his rasping voice describe the way a whale carcass sinks to the cold, heavy waters, and as it decays fuels a whole community of organisms, creatures so far from the surface they don't need sunlight, but flourish in that strange element. The slow transfiguration of flesh into this new phase, this new state of decay and invention. The whale decays, but that does not mean it's annihilated. A gospel of transfiguration, he said, knowing she would like his word choice.

A person may blet as well, Judith announced to Wurtzel, her cat — a kitten she had found after Ben died — just as a whale falls. Just as Ben fell and undertook the alchemical transformations of all matter. The Institute did not choose to use that language in the email she received, confirming her candidacy for the Procedure. The day she received the confirmation, she carried a medlar in from the back porch to the little sunroom, Judith sat and spooned up the brown mush that spilled out of the skin — rendered flavorless by her illness — and tried to conjure Ben's voice saying, *you know what that looks like, Jude?* Medlars are composite creatures of rot and stillness, flesh transfigured by time, fragrant like apple blossoms and ferment on the tongue.

She'd have to find someone to take Wurtzel. Someone who'd let him outside in the middle of the night when he was restless, and who would not require too much affection, but let him creep closer and closer to them as they sat on the couch watching TV, knowing when to stroke him diffidently, with just one finger.

You are already colonized, she had said to Wurtzel, and your lineaments are temporary. You have already taken on many shapes, a bud, and a bloom, and a fruit, and then you will fall, and turn gold, and brown, and your flesh will find new forms and long after your death. And what follows on that? Only more of the same.

✦

The man. The man. He was wrong. He had said it wouldn't hurt because of Pentobarbitol. But it hurt and they wouldn't tell her anything. She threw up. She threw up again.

She had done everything right. It was supposed to be —

— she threw up.

She threw up and it seemed, this time, that her body was trying to expel itself, peristalsis tearing apart her alimentary canal, as though it could reorganize the body that contained it. Not a snake swallowing its tail, but its inverse, a snake turning inside out. Then there was blood, black and thick. The girl who came with tea that morning — 10ml syringes of cool peppermint tea gave her some relief from the taste of blood — would not look at her. There were no longer any mirrors in her room, so she did not know what the girl saw, only that it must be strange and awful.

"Help me," Judith said.

The girl started as though she had not expected speech. Judith reached out her hand which — she could see — seemed thinner than it had been, the bones apparent, the flesh sunken and grey at the fingernails. "Will you," she said, "help me?"

Her eyes fixed on the window, the girl set down the tray just out of Judith's reach. "Help me," Judith said again. The girl seemed not to hear, and keeping her eyes averted, she tapped her watch. The hallway filled with a low, musical alarm.

"Please."

The girl left. Judith struggled onto her side and reached for the syringe. Swallowed tea — green and fragrant with mint —

then spit it all up, the cup covered with a dark red-brown smear. Oh. She thought. This must be it.

Then three figures in white suits opened the door, their faces covered by masks, and she felt herself lifted onto a gurney.

"Is Sadik there? I want Sadik," she said to them. They were shouting.

Then she was in the corpse garden, walking and crawling along the winding paths, past sensors and bodies, with whitesuits following behind. She observed in loving detail the other geonauts, their slight movements, their limbs overtaken by mushrooms or the white roots of grass or submerged in an ant hill built industriously over their face, another sunk in water, green-eyed with algae. Their movements were slow, like the movements of plants in response to sunlight. One individual, their skin covered in luminous green moss, rose up onto an elbow, and Judith saw the white roots and potato bugs that colonized the earth beneath their shoulder. Mouth working open and closed as though they were saying something she could not hear, some discourse on the nature of transformation, and the world they perceived through decaying eyes. The only thing that emerged from their mouth was a trickle of earwigs.

"How do you feel?" Sadik asked, his voice a surprise in the darkness where her face rested against the trunk of a tree. She felt the heat of his hand on her shoulder and wondered how long he had been there.

"I think we'd better do it soon," she said. Maybe she said it. "I'm as ready as I'm ever going to be."

"Judith —"

Sadik, she realized for the first time, was wearing a white suit and a mask. There were two people in suits standing back. They were stupid if they thought that made a difference.

Judith took a step. She took a step. She took a step. The young whitesuits were afraid. It was all over for them, those fast-moving and disconnected creatures, blind agents of something much larger and more complex, from which their speed and cleverness separated them. None of them understood, surface dwellers. She stared at an intersection of white roots and quartz, ruffled with lichen.

One crusted finger traced the lichen over granite. This was a good place, high enough that she could see over the walls and to the Pacific, as far as Japan if she listened hard to the emerging noise of Radio Mycorrhiza.

"Have you ever eaten a medlar?" she asked, and rainwater fell from her fingers.

"I don't think so." Though he had seemed calm, when he spoke his voice shuddered. That was Sadik. Quick, she thought, with an audibly beating heart, and blood that rushed like river water through supple veins.

It was dark. Her fingers were powdered green, which despite her blindness, she saw, as she saw a pale flame consuming the rock, and her body with a chorus of whispers. She was naked. Lichen spilled over her chin to her lip, she could taste it. Water and stone, peaty and slow-living. She would have closed her eyes, but she found she did not need to do that, either, so she lay back against the stone she had chosen, and felt one arm give against it, which should hurt, but didn't, then the arm gave way and she tumbled down the boulder, and something wet cracked deep inside her skull. She came to rest facing up, and through the dimming green haze she had her last human glimpse of the stars.

Lichen covered her teeth and crept down her throat. Sometime later she felt her limbs consumed by underground creatures, greedy things, eating their way through her skin, where her body touched the earth.

She tasted rock and the resinous needles of the Sitka spruce, low-growing and bonsaied by the raw little island. During long damp nights she turned her face to follow the moon, even when her eyes were gone, and her sockets grown over with lichen. The beetles crawled over her skin. The beetles crawled through her skin. Then something with many legs rippled where her eyes had been. There was water around her feet. The moon was a lady's slipper. The moon was full and golden. The air was cold and warm and dry and rain-filled.

Who are you? she asked in what remained of her brain, that network of intersecting electrical currents now intersecting with other networks made of entwining rhizomorphs, hyphae, her breached skin, her thickened blood, filled now with Actino-mycetales, richly seething with microscopic life. A Judith-shaped collective that now lived in the cage of her bones. Through them, she heard the glitter and hiss of the underworld's language. And now, it seemed, she understood some of its intent. Somewhere, someone was calling to her along tree roots and mycelia, so she could hear — at the horizon of audibility — other geonauts, an underworld, an afterlife.

✦

When Ben died, Judith still talked to him. Several people suggested it was evidence of an afterlife, like she must know with a widow's piercing insight that something of him survived physical death, and hung around the corners of his old life. She did not believe them, though she conversed with him about her diagnosis, and Wurtzel, and her decision to come to the island. She scolded him for not taking better care and taking another month, two months, a year, with her. She pointed out changes, where new waves lapped the sidewalks, and told him that the basements of

Victoria-by-the-Sea flooded during bad storms. She told him that a child was born entirely devoid of microbial companions, and that the child died of anaphylaxis within three hours of birth. She confided only to him when she began to forget things in a way that scared her. Once when she was shopping and couldn't figure out how she got where she was — having turned right out of the parking lot instead of left, because of traffic — she talked through it with him, until she found a map on her phone and remembered how to read it, doing what he would have done.

✦

From the corpse garden, the bletted woman rose. She could not say how long she had spent pressed into the earth, only that it was long enough to have been transfigured by those companions that had lived in her gut and her sinuses and under her fingernails her whole life, which had overtaken the body they previously only cohabited. While she had never been alone — no one is ever alone — she now knew those companions intimately, and the creature who rose from the earth knew itself to be composite. As it had always been composite.

It was good to lend her human shape to the underworld, and so allow the other orders to communicate with the ascendant predators of the planet. As Ben had temporarily lent his shape to a community of sea creatures just outside the Gulf of St Lawrence. A vector for newness. A human-shaped interface for the microbial world. We can talk to them, with our human-shaped mouths, and our human hands, and this thin scrim of human-shaped longing that covers over the truth, which is the underworld of the minuscule.

The ones above ground? They're afraid.

The being who tore herself out of the roots and the under sur-face of beetles began to walk from her granite perch — where she had set herself, decades before — was something new, though she bore the imprint of Judith, her lineaments and her memories.

There were lots of them. One who had been there the longest walked with a tree grown deeply into their core, host and parasite both, entwined bones and flesh and rot and insect and larvae and root and rhizomorph and memory and language. Three bodies had fused together, limbs entangled and torsos compressed, walking crabwise on arms and legs and heads, dragging some limbs, and dragged along by others. It was good to be close to one another, no distinction between the earth that contains you, that teems with mites and monsters and microbial films, and the body that — for a while at least — might serve as interface for all those microscopic beings and processes. Rot, Judith had once said, is a valid state of affairs.

The shambling body that had once been Judith's exclusive and isolated home was green with the feathery dust of lichen. She incu-bated the rich miasma of the new kind, incompatible with the fast-moving, glittering creatures on the other side of the glass of the observation deck. She thought it had been different, once, full of white light and activity, and now dark and nearly empty, but for those frightened bodies overhead.

All you poor orphans in a changing world, you should listen to what the dead are saying, because the new world won't tolerate you. Having borrowed the human faculty of speech, and the tech-nologies of language, she lent the network the only suitable word she could remember from her human life, and heard it go up in a global chorus, over mycorrhizal networks, yes, but also to data processing centers, and out into the cloud, as it was still known. She spoke it, or it spoke her, all over the world: ARISE.

Poor unrooted creatures. Judith — green lichened Judith — raised her hand and undertook the last recognizably human action of her existence. She opened the door. Inside she found them all, lucid with terror, watching. Among them, the Judith-thing saw a familiar face, though changed by fear and time. She wished to tell him what she knew, but she did not think he would understand, so instead she put her arms around him and drew him close to her bones.

Story Notes

This is among the worst futures I can imagine for the world — a surveillance dystopia without privacy or secrets, where the state is consolidating total control over our internal lives. I set it in a place I know well, so I can imagine the changes more intimately, and feel the contrast between our present world and what it might become. The desolate landscape through which Mar drives feels very close sometimes, its droughts and wildfires seem like the inevitable fallout of the present. The difference is that in Mar's world there is no escape, no road you can follow into the woods, no possibility for change. There is only the state, and the tiny areas of resistance that people can create for themselves, in their relationships with others, and in their secrets.

In many ways, this science fictional future draws on Canada's imperial and corporate past, back when we were subjects of both the British empire and the Hudson's Bay Company. Here, though, the natural world is utterly defeated, and the new site of colonization is the human heart.

Such Thoughts Are Unproductive

The woman whom I sometimes believed to be my mother flickered. Once. Twice. A cloud of pixels, and her face frozen in a smile, while her arm — the wide-ranging gestures that were as much a marker of her identity as the color of her eyes or her fingerprints — swept the screen, leaving blue eddies, whirlpools of information. Then silence, but her mouth moved, leaving a flesh-colored smudge across the top half of her head.

"You've cut out again," I said.

The picture reset. She was saying something that made her laugh.

"Your hair looks really good," I said.

"Wha —"

I waited. Repeated myself.

"Yes," she said, suddenly clear, "I cut it myself because the guy they get in is terrible. He let me use his scissors, at least. So chic and DIY. If it was 2015 I'd pin it —"

Slide show, for which I was paying five dollars a minute. Figures in black pacing against the yellow cinder block wall of the common room. I tried not to look at them because it was always better not to look at them. It was better when I could see the windows, and get a look at where she was.

"We're running out of time," I said. "I only paid for fifteen minutes, cause last time you had the drill and I thought maybe —"

The hand, now trailing pixels. It was definitely her face, but I searched her jawline for the suture where her appearance had been attached, virtually, to this body, a scrim of pixels over the person that was — as far as anything was these days — my mother. Her smile. Her expressive hands. No matter how empty the content of our words, there was comfort in seeing her speak.

I could not, though, let go of the suspicion that this face I was searching — hanging again, lag deforming the number on her grey uniformed shoulder — was not my mother, so much as the collected fragments of her from a hundred thousand hours of CCTV footage and intercepted video conferences and texts and whatever other material had streamed through the state's huge filter-feeding machines, snuffling all traffic — dark and light, private or public — for the information it required on problematic —

— Such thoughts are unproductive.

This woman I speak to, who is my mother, and who may not be my mother, fills the space in my life called mother. I will continue to chat with her when I can because the illusion — if it is an illusion — is so close to reality that sometimes I am taken in and relax into daughterly affection.

The black silhouettes in the background of the common room do nothing to interfere with our conversation because no part of our conversation can be hidden from the eye that watches us all, which is not an eye, but the hundred thousand eyes of a filter-feeding behemoth made entirely of information. She sends me messages at night, long discourses on the problem of making the food palatable, or the solitaire she plays, or the Scrabble tournaments she organizes. I can hear the powerful gears of her mind grinding against the cinder block walls of the place, finding things to put in order, to make, to fix. Her resources are limited: games and other companions, the discussions and lectures and regular chastisement that she undergoes, which she does not mention, but which is always implied. I can imagine her turning that mind toward the problem of 2 + 2 being 5, producing the right answer for the individuals who ask her — daily, hourly, by the minute — to repeat this new truth. A problem of philosophy? Perhaps of language, she would say, from the perspective of new-radical-orthodoxy, or neo-post-Platonism. One needs only adjust the definitions in that portion of one's brain that is cordoned off from reality in order to comply with the ideologies of the state. That's how she gives the right answer without dying of it.

She never says these things. The mother who exists in my mind — which might or might not align with the mother on the screen, or in my messages — would do such things. It would be necessary for her survival, once the small collection of paper books were arranged by the Library of Congress system, with gaps on the shelf for "critical theory" and "resistance" and "escape plans."

But what kind of escape could she possibly need? The enclosures are beautiful, despite the yellow cinder block walls. I've seen them when her back is to the window. I've seen the trees and mountains outside. When I was a kid, we often drove through the Rockies and stopped at Banff. Once we stayed in a massive chateau on Lake Louise. There were men and women in lederhosen outside, playing alphorns. The air, when we left the sticky lowland fug of our car — was so fresh and lovely I wanted to cry. The glaciers had receded, but you could still see the blue-white glow of them up high, far beyond us.

I think — I'm not sure — but I think I have seen similar mountains in the brief moments she directs the camera over her shoulder and out the window. The time zone can't be too far different, just much farther north, because the summer nights are bright. Toad River, I think. One of the big Provincial Parks. I have looked at maps — old ones on paper, tearing at the folds — and

141

seen the gaps in the satellite images, and I have wondered, is she there? Close to 60?

This winter I'll watch the angles of sunlight and track the darkness behind her. I'll hope she picks up on my questions: I've had trouble with my nasturtiums again. Are you growing anything? And hope she turns her camera toward the window.

◆

We live in an age of infinitely preserved information, so it's not actually odd that I save every video call on an external hard drive. At night I turn off the Wi-Fi and study the files, trying to remember how to identify a fake, but I don't search for "ten ways to spot a fake" because that leaves fingerprints, and we all know that I'm a problematic citizen, confirmed as such by my associations rather than any action I have taken. To be visible means you have done something to deserve visibility, after all. And if our exploration of the human genome has taught us anything, it is that my genes are treacherous.

You can inherit treachery, or be infected with it, by the people who wait in government offices, slouching from hard blue chair to hard blue chair, and sharing between them the rumors and possibilities regarding what happened to the missing. Camps. Education centers. Wilderness highways that stop dead on the other side of the great divide. The blank spots that are slowly overtaking Google Earth, even archived versions I thought I had kept safe. No more news from Fort McMurray, not for a couple of years now. The pipelines never leak. Silence accompanies any disruption of gasoline, or the regular oil spills up and down the Salish Sea, where all the fish are dead. There's another dam on the Peace River to celebrate, but the blackouts still get worse.

When I have thoroughly and silently examined the information available to me (is that a tamarack? A black spruce? Is that a mountain?), it occurs to me that since the woman I talk to might be scrimmed with my mother's face, so might the room in which she sits. The darkness and light I have so painstakingly tracked, the faint, blue line of a mountain, and a pink winter sunset at three in the afternoon? That may well mean nothing. Worse than nothing: deception.

At work I am also a watcher. I sanity check the AI that surveils traffic errors in the western provinces. I look for anomalies and find ways to integrate them into the AI's understanding. I am slowly eliminating my own job, because the anomalies are rarer and rarer as the world becomes more and more perfectly known. I have thought, sometimes, following on my father's philosophical leanings, that this is the goal of our state: perfect knowledge of landscapes and people and relationships. So perfect that the simulacrum we see on the screen is, like the system I manage, more perfect than the territory we possess. The woman on the screen is my mother, as is the woman in my messages, so perfectly has she been synthesized by the state that also slit —

— Unproductive.

◆

"Have you heard from da —"

"— He's okay. Did you get that? You're a slideshow."

"Weak —"

I was a slideshow, too. Maybe she didn't even think it was me. Maybe there was another woman she spoke to mid-week, and she believed that was the real daughter, and she only spoke to me because the system required her to maintain the fiction. Maybe she had a million daughters asking her leading questions. Maybe.

Still smiling, in case we connect, I wrote on my tablet and held it up to my phone: HE'S STILL WORKING ON THE SOLAR PANELS. Dad withdrew from the city to our old cabin in the interior (is she near there? Farther north and east. The forests I have seen out that window are deep and green), when Mom left, or disappeared, or was taken, whichever mode you choose to use for description. Dad and I just say "when Mom left" like it's the only date that matters. He hasn't come back to the city since. I took two weeks off work to help him chuck their things, and carry what was important — photographs, old books, her clothes, her jewelry — to the cabin. We couldn't afford to take much, with the cost of gas. The house was requisitioned later, for a nominal fee that didn't cover the time or energy it would have taken him to get the papers signed. I don't go by the house anymore. I don't like to see it.

"Do you remember when we camped at Banff?"

"When you graduated from high school? Or are you talking about before Sophie's wedding?"

"Sophie? Piano teacher? At Banff?"

"Aunt Sophie, not piano Sophie. We were roommates all through grad school. If you were going to have a godmother, she would have been your godmother. You were pretty little that trip, though."

I remember Banff, because we went right up to the glacier and Dad showed me where it had been each year, walking backward through time, saying *this is when you were born* and *this is when I was born.*

"I was like five? Four? I thought that was Emily's wedding."

"No, Sophie. And I was maid of honor so I had to be there three days early, and you and Daddy ate junk food and went on the swings until you threw up. You hated Fudgsicles for a year after that summer. I should have done that with more junk food. You'd be vegan now."

◆

I actually am vegan. I do not remember having an aunt named Sophie. I'm pretty sure it was Emily's wedding. Dad and I played on the merry-go-round until we were so dizzy we stumbled across the soccer field toward the edge of the forest, collapsing on the grass until the world stopped spinning and we'd expelled all the Doritos and gummy worms we'd eaten. That afternoon, Mom — woozy and white-faced after a late night — got ready in a blue dress I had never seen before, her hair up high and her makeup all pretty. She carried me into this old lodge halfway up the mountain, and shouted over my shoulder to friends I had seen in pictures, but never met, making jokes about things I didn't understand. Dad and I left during the dancing, but she came in long after that, laughing. She slept in late, grouchy, cuddling a water bottle to her pillow, while we went driving in search of coffee and hot chocolate. "And what do you say to more Doritos, Mar?" Dad asked, and I pretended to throw up.

In that conversation, Mom said other things that left me watchful and adrenalized. I didn't draw attention to the discrepancies because her memory might be flawed, but so was mine. So was everyone's, except the filter-feeding behemoth that follows us all, and while we didn't seem to possess the same past, it possessed us equally. For more than a year I didn't hear from her, not even to confirm she still existed. I waited patiently in offices, both virtual queues and in person, and I went to Victoria to line up with all the others at the Ministry of Information Management and Retrieval. The answers were always the same: here's a chit with a number. We'll be in touch. Said with a synthetic smile by an AI phone tree, or a tired clerk behind glass. They will always get back to you.

I am patient and consistent, also better connected than a lot of people, so I have pushed further than most. I also know the system better, and know when to leave things be, keep my head down, be grateful that I know my mother is alive. I am the model supplicant, waiting in dove-like patience outside the walls for the emergence of her mother, whose radical spirit has been (will be) corrected by the benevolent ministrations of the state.

✦

You got to know other people because you saw them at the offices and in the spillover corridors. Which wasn't to say you *know* them, just that you were familiar with their face and their concerns. Julie's looking for her brother and nephews. Chris wants to find his wife. Chris thinks she's in the foothills somewhere. Alberta has a few sites. You avoided the ones with loud voices who listed all the possible explanations, even the ones you shouldn't say out loud: they have been replaced by bots of some description; their minds are being damaged beyond coherence by electroshock or DBS. Uncommon, but appealing: discrepancies are coded messages that only family will recognize, and thus communicate important information about location, and security movements, and the details of what's happening inside, in preparation for a massive action. We should all pool the discrepancies and see what picture they show us, if we stand far enough back. We should talk. We should organize.

I have never contributed to these efforts. In lineups — the sorts of lineups that involve standing up every fifteen minutes to move one spot down in the long row of hard blue chairs — I listened, but said nothing, only thought, *you don't know how loud your voice is why don't you care that the walls are full of cameras and your face is so intimately known to the machine no one you love can ever be sure it's you talking to them.*

I didn't need specifics regarding what happened inside, because what happened inside is what's happened inside such education centers since they were first invented. Repetition and regulation. Rote recitation of truths regarding the nature of the society to which we belong. The principle being — I knew this, because Mom told me — that the surface recitation has a transformative effect on the mind, even if the mind resists the meaning of the words it says.

And then the experiments, and the strategic application of pain —

"— Recite platitudes that deny climate change," she said, "or the refugee crisis or ethnic cleansing or forced sterilization or eugenics. The perfectibility of the human animal in an ideal society. Repeat it and eventually you believe it. Or act like you believe it, which is just as good as far as they're concerned."

That was near the end, when she said those sorts of things out loud, and in text, and every last fragment collected and shared across whatever the network is now. Five Eyes. Nine Eyes. Ten Billion Eyes. In collaboration, those systems extracted meaning and implication from the marks she made on the screens and the sounds from her mouth — rarely out of range of a microphone — cross-referencing those patterns with other patterns. They flagged her profile. They saw the outcomes, and identified my mother as a point of vulnerability. In her terms: an imperfect citizen.

Me too, probably, and Dad, though we're less threatening. We don't talk often anymore. It's difficult to have a conversation when most of what matters is dangerous to say out loud. Dad mentions that he's repainting the garage. I talk about how I want to do a bike trip through Oregon. Dad says he thinks he's got a rat in the basement. I say I had some decent wontons at a new place that opened around the corner. Hanging over our conversation, a list of things we don't mention: droughts (unless historical); disappearing island chains; climate refugees; the rage associated with rising temperatures and food prices; the —

— But this isn't productive. We both know. We talk about whether he can catch the rat with a humane trap. We talk about how smart rats are, and how deftly they have adapted to human landscapes. I say I'll make a trip to help. He says no no, no need. I'm fine. I say, you should come visit me, do city stuff, and he says no no no, no need. I'm fine. We're both fine. As you can see, I am now good at lying.

I ran into an aunt at some event, and she said, "I haven't heard from your Mom in *ages*, how is she?"

"Oh. She's doing better."

"Better? What happened?"

"She contracted one of the antibiotic-resistant strains of TB, and she's taking some time to recover."

"I'm so sorry to hear it. Where is she?"

"One of the new sanitoriums. She'll be in for a while."

"Oh, Mar. She'll be in my thoughts. Pass that on, would you? Or maybe I'll email her."

This was the safe response. An innocuous message passed on. No further inquiry. No possibility of betrayal.

✦

I set my keys on the little shelf by the door and sighed, the way you do when you take off high heels, or get somewhere quiet where you can cry. Then I heard someone shifting on my couch.

She squealed. "Mar! Mar! Look at you! The last time I saw you was at your Mom's fiftieth. When was that? Oh god don't tell me. That means we're old."

I have an aunt Sophie. She was a thin, athletic woman, honey-brown hair, not mom's pixie cut, but of the same vintage, choppy, with playful silver highlights. She was dressed in elegant athleisure. And you know, at that moment she could have been an aunt, one of the women from Mom's PhD program, or a second cousin, or someone from the Elder college where she taught political philosophy.

✦

"Where did you —?"

"— I'm going to be in town for a couple of weeks, and I'm going to be nearby while I deal with a contract. I saw your Mom, you know."

"What?"

"Last week. That's why I'm here. I knew you were in the city, but I didn't know where, obviously, and — okay, I was a little embarrassed that I've been so out of touch with everyone. It's these short contracts. They're disorienting. I travel. So. Much."

"You heard from mom?"

"Yes. And I realized how much I've missed of your life these last years. Remember when I lived on Elm Street and you guys used to come over and we'd go to that one park with the splash pad, and then we'd get ice cream on the Drive?"

I found myself nodding. It's what you do. Lie.

"Anyway," my new aunt said. "I thought I'd come over, and I had your Mom's key so. I brought you dinner, too. Are you still vegan?"

"Yes," I said. "For five years now."

"Good. You know, while I was waiting I remembered how much you hated cooking when you were a teenager — remember how your Mom tried to teach you to make, I don't know, spaghetti sauce and the fights you had. Oh God. I heard about the fights."

I had not remembered those fights in years. "The bolognese," I said. "I still can't make it. On principle."

"I brought pakoras. They're off the fucking hook — I ate like two of them waiting for you. Let's go eat the rest."

The pakoras were excellent. The rice she also brought was fragrant and nutty underneath the curry. The beer delicious, bubbling out of our glasses and over the rough table on my back deck, that just had room for four people. Sophie talked about grad school and Mom, about parties they threw together, about staying up late crying over deadlines and supervisors, about graduation, and how Mom had blown hers off for the government job, but had been there the next year for Sophie's, already pregnant with me.

"So you were at my graduation. Good luck charm."

I slid into this the way we slid into so many things: the loss of cities to the encroaching waters and deserts, the swamps and the new virus creeping north along the Mississippi, as the days grew hotter and the mosquitoes adapted. A kind of compliant quiet — pleasant, safe — overtook me as I thought yes, of course I had an aunt named Sophie. Of course.

She slept that night on the couch. It was the obvious thing to do. Curfew.

That night I lay in bed and recited the facts of my life: I do not have an aunt named Sophie; my mother did not have antibiotic resistant TB and was not in a sanitorium on one of the quarantine islands. My mother is in an internment camp with yellow cinder block walls, somewhere in the mountains, far enough north that she's surrounded by tamarack, maybe by black spruce. At the end of the road with no exit. Britney is gone. The dam on the Peace River was bombed last year. Gasoline shortages are worse.

In the dark I texted Mom, or the Mom-function of some bot, or the person assigned to be my Mom that shift, while my real Mom — the internal enemy — underwent her daily re-education, which wasn't happening but was happening all the time. Maybe, I thought, as I typed, these words are shuttling right out to the living room, where my aunt Sophie was not sleeping, but surveilling the various fictions of my family relationships. I wondered how many nieces and nephews she had.

Sophie is here.

Who? Came the answer, too quickly, maybe she wasn't sleeping. She had trouble sleeping, she said, despite all the fresh air and exercise.

Sophie. My aunt.

Awesome. How is she? I haven't seen her for ages. She asked about you, though. Not surprised she turned up. She just finished that contract in Halifax.

She's great. She brought pakoras from the place on Main.

Oh man. I miss those.

They're really good. We have leftovers. I wish we could send them.

I want potstickers from Hon's. And honeymoon rice. Then we should go for gelato.

Triple scoop. Then back for another three.

You should ask your Dad if he'll come into town and have gelato with you.

He's so busy.

I didn't write *he hates the city now* or *he hates people now* or *neither of us can afford the gas if we want to eat*. I wrote, *he's so busy* and somewhere, the mom-function, or the behemoth, took note.

Have you heard from Britney?

And then I had to stop, because the question hurt so much it didn't matter whether the woman on the other side was my mother, or a fiction, or some synthesis of true and false too complicated to understand.

✦

You ask yourself as you read my record: why is she so compliant? Why doesn't she tell the woman who keeps visiting daily, bringing food and asking questions about work and dating and mom and dad, why doesn't she just say, you aren't my aunt, I don't have an aunt.

I answer: because this is what we all do. Because I don't want to end up removed to a complex somewhere in the northern mountains, where if I escaped the hundreds of km between me and a highway would kill me before any of the guards had to. Because things can always get worse for everyone involved. Because they need someone on the outside.

But also. Also. Because she knows that I love honeymoon rice, and that I would like nothing better than to gorge on pakoras and gelato with Mom and Dad, and talk about inconsequential things, without reference to —— or —— or ——, but rather what we watched on TV and whether it was a Mac's convenience or a 7-Eleven that we used to stop at on our way out of town for holiday road trips (it was definitely a 7-Eleven). Whether the aphids are back on the nasturtiums. I talk this way with the entity who is/is not my mother, who may be my mother, who may be human. The entity behaves so exactly like my mother, and I like that, because then I don't think about how she's dead, or in solitary, somewhere, with the volume cranked to 79 decibels on prog rock or economic propaganda —

— But this is not productive.

My face betrays itself to the camera that is watching me, that also hears the catch in my voice when I thank the barista for my coffee. I use the drive-through because it offers marginally more privacy, since it can't read your whole body, and because if you order with the app the drink is there and you don't have to say

anything and you have the pleasure of silence, though your face —
the breathing, roughened by repressed tears — is still visible to it.

The girl who gives me my drink is impassive, but I think — a
flicker of sympathy in her eyes? She can't tell that I'm contaminated by my association with my mother, that I have an Aunt
Sophie. But maybe she's contaminated, too, and has an Aunt
Sophie. Who knows. You don't wait long enough to find out.

Sophie and I watch movies and go for walks, and sometimes I
think how much I would like it if Sophie was my aunt. She clucks
over me when I cough, and asks whether I've tried turmeric and
makes me tea of mint and ginger. It would be very easy to accept
the gentleness of this state-sponsored intervention, ignoring the
deviations I hear in conversation, and the fact that she is also
someone else's aunt. I like Sophie. That's what I keep thinking. I
like her. I like having someone sort of like a Mom around, check-
ing in, asking leading questions about work.

We walk past my neighbors who say, who's that, Mar? And I
say, this is my Aunt Sophie, and they all smile, and I don't know
— not really — if they believe me, or if Aunt has become code for
them as it has for me, for something you can't talk about, a person
who is close to you like a missing lover, like family, but who is —

— unproductive.

✦

Dad called. Unusual, therefore treacherous. "It's confirmed," he
said.

Sophie was on the porch. She'd waved yes yes when I got the
call. Take it. But I'll just keep eating. I'd made us cold noodles with
mint leaves and basil from the pot I kept in the corner of the little
deck.

"When?"

"This morning. I'm going to head out tomorrow morning."

"I could be there —"

"— No, you can't. It's contagious. You'll have to get checked out. They'll be in touch. Probably soon."

"What do you need?"

"Nothing. Just to hear your voice."

In the silence of my throat shutting — and on the other side of the line, his throat shutting too — I tried to think of safe things I could say. But all expression is evidence.

"What is it?"

"TB." He paused. "You know the one."

We all knew what that meant. There's nothing for us to say, because probably all the feelings, all the fear and anger were exhausted that first year when we didn't hear from Mom, and he went with me to the offices with the hard blue chairs. Now, though, it was the familiar and inexorable creep of the end as all us imperfect citizens were taken up, one by one.

Sophie started as soon as I hung up the phone, "What happened?"

I said nothing.

"Talk to me, honey."

Mom used to call me honey. She still did sometimes, in text. Sometimes she didn't.

"It's your Dad, isn't it. I know how hard this is."

I threw things into my pack. T-shirts. Socks. Solar charger. Filter bottle. Fleece.

"You can't go silent on me. Mar. Mar. Do you think this is what your mother wants? Seriously? You have to talk."

Documents, hidden from her view by the closed door, on which she banged her fists, tucked into my waistband.

"It's not good to bottle everything up inside. You need to learn to trust people."

My backpack — the giant frame one that Dad got me for my first real solo expedition, the summer I was twenty. It cost twice what I wanted, but he insisted, and he'd been right because here it still was. I checked my balance with Humanitas, the telecom provider for all the camps. Sanitoriums. Whatever. Ten minutes banked against next week's call, and enough for a handful of texts, so I hit dial.

She didn't answer. I rang again, just swallowing the five dollars. Then the woman appeared, her back to the windows.

"Hey, I didn't expect —"

The image of my mother-not-mother hung, and reflexively I studied the margins of her face for the suture between reality and interference, the faint betraying lines of an AI's adjustment.

"You cut out."

"I didn't expect to hear from you. I heard from your Dad yesterday, though, so both of you are off schedule. What's up?"

"Dad's sick."

The image hung. I picked up the jiffy I had ready in case, and began writing on the white wall of my bedroom. DAD IS SICK I AM GOING TO VISIT HIM.

Her face hanging in the moment that she understood what I wrote — animated only by the shimmer of pixels across my screen. She might have dropped, but I kept my phone fixed on the wall. One way or another, they already knew, and if it was Mom. If it was. If. Then she had to know.

"Are you talking to her? Is that her?" Sophie shouted. "You can't disturb her recovery, Mar. That's selfish. That's just fucking *selfish*."

She said other things in quick succession, about my being a bad daughter, about how I was a bitch, about how I shouldn't be so hard on myself, careening from insult to affection in a split second in order to stop me from doing — something. I wondered if she'd try to hit me.

I locked up the apartment with Sophie still following me, talking about opening up, saying are you a fucking rock? Tell me what's wrong with Bastien, he's my friend too, you can't shut me out. A thousand other platitudes about sharing the burden of pain.

I got into the car. She stood in front of it.

"Why don't you just put a tracker on me," I said, "and let me go. It'll all be over soon anyway."

"I don't know what you're talking about."

I inched forward. She leaned onto the hood and I thought, this may be the single stupidest moment of my entire life.

"We're family, Mar."

Maybe she told the truth, though not in the way she thought. We were family in the sense that we were bound to the same omnivorous machine. I could hear her saying those words to someone else, someone standing behind me, someone looking out of my eyes, and I wanted to say, *who is it? Who are you talking to?*

I unlocked the door. She got in, face full of rage-tears.

"You can't rescue him," she said. "You need to trust that things happen for a reason."

◆

I thought about killing her. I thought about killing myself. I thought about driving into the roadblock at the exit for Needle Park, which was now manned by American uniforms, hazmat suits, trucks with Chinese plates. But while I often have those thoughts, I have never pursued them. It's how I have survived as long as I have, why I haven't been scooped with my parents, with Brit —

— But thinking of Britney would make things even worse than they were. So instead I thought about the roadblocks, and how the exits for Kingsvale and Brookmere and Coldwater were bulldozed, so you couldn't leave the car to feel the air change as you climb into the mountains.

She talked. She laughed. She told the same stories about my mother in grad school, what a mess she was during her comps, cleaning the bathroom at midnight, smoking until dawn on their tiny, rotten front porch. Ha ha ha.

I thought of all the times we started our summer road trips on the Coquihalla, headed to the cabin, or farther north and east. Other years due south along the American coast, watching the beaches change from shingle to sand, to Manzanita and Tillamook, then farther south until we found our way to California. I thought of camping, and the dogs with me in the back seat.

Her throat raw with talk, she said, "Your parents love you so much." She said, "They want what's best for you, and what's best is to let them get better."

"We're going to need gas," I said. "I'll stop at Merritt."

"Are you even listening? I'm here because I love you, Mar, and because I'm trying to convince you to move on with your life, and let them go. You can't change this."

Once, a year ago, when I still hadn't heard from Mom, and Dad had just moved to the interior but was off the grid because of the fires and the Coquihalla was still roadblocked because of the attack on the dam, and I had no idea about anything anymore, and Britney was —

— I had the opportunity to find an aunt, or a niece, or a cousin. This happens when when you appear to be as compliant as I am. Ashley — my direct manager — called me into a meeting with someone I'd never seen before, a woman in a sleek grey suit who talked about how I could help Britney and my mother and anyone else I cared to help, by telling them about my extended family, about those cousins I met sometimes on the hard blue chairs. I told them I didn't have any cousins like that, but that I'd think about it. I wondered, later, if my hesitation was enough. Maybe we were all damned because I thought instead of saying, yes yes whatever you like I'll find a cousin and tell you anything you need to know.

The lineup at the gas station was shorter than it was in Vancouver. Thirty minutes. I thought of killing her again, my aunt Sophie, who had grown so familiar to me, messenger from a childhood I had not had, a life I did not lead in a country that no longer existed, full of loving familiar bonds, and gentle teasing, and a father not slowly dying of TB, a mother not being tortured by —

— I said, "There has to be someone you're protecting, right?"

"You, Mar. You're my goddaughter," she said it mechanically, and I could imagine the dialogue somewhere in the dossier that archived me, identified my vulnerabilities, catalogued my failures. I have no godmother, no aunt, no mother, no wife. "I swore at your christening that I would uphold the ethical and social bond of our relationship. That I would love you. I promised —"

— We moved a car length forward. You could smell the wildfires, and see last year's burnout, overgrown with fireweed.

"Daughter?" I asked. "Your sister? Granddaughter?"

It was like a moonscape out there, Dad said when he drove through after the fires. On the other side of the mountain, the cabin was safe, but probably not for many more seasons. I had always thought that I could escape there, if I needed to, get the camping gear, and walk out to some place no one will ever set foot. A mountain. A valley where I could wait until this was over.

"You should probably go see them," I said. "Whoever they are. They'd rather see you than get whatever help you think they'll get. Because you're not helping. Not really."

When we got to the pump I filled up, then we went in to pay and get some water, and whatever candy was available because that's what you do in Merritt, you get snacks for the last two hours on the road, even if they were sparse and overpriced gummy worms.

She said, "You know I don't have a choice."

I nodded.

"She's not your mother, probably, the one you talk to. You know where your mother is. You know what they do."

I nodded.

"I did actually know your parents in grad school. I did. You were in utero at my graduation. That's why they thought — And I was already doing. It. This. For her. I was doing it because if I don't —"

— And I will grant her a little privacy here. It only takes a few words when it's people like us, the imperfect citizens of this perfectly known world. She told me things I do not wish to know, because they hurt to know, then we both looked instinctively for cameras and drones and microphones.

She said, "I have to go to the lady's."

I went back to the car, and drank from the water bottle, then started the engine. A full tank of gas, the sunlight brilliant, and I pulled out of the lot. I had, I figured, a couple of hours before they got to me, and by then, I would be at Dad's, and maybe we could talk for a few minutes before they came. I saw the signs for Peachland and Kelowna, and the sun was going down, and eating the gummy worms I could almost be on one of those other road trips, out from the city to the cabin for a week, or maybe past the mountains and somewhere else, north maybe. This time I'd make Britney come with us, even if I had to beg her to take time away from work. And — the image came to me though I did not want it

— Sophie with us, sitting up late to talk with mom. I could imagine another lifetime in which she was my aunt, when she and her daughter might have joined us for a week on the lake, drinking beer by the water, and swatting at the mosquitoes together.

Story Notes

Salmon forests are miraculous. They also resist storytelling. How do you talk about a network that ignores our ordinary divisions between land and ocean? That includes the abyssal depths of the Bering Sea and the tops of Douglas fir trees far inland? In very real, material ways, salmon created the landscape of the coastal north Pacific, and thousands of plants, animals, microbes, and fungi depend on salmon eaten, digested, excreted, taken up, and transfigured into new bodies. I'm still not sure how to write about something so large, so important, and so elusive. No single salmon is the salmon forest — each plant, body, or stream is only one part of the huge transoceanic flow of energy.

While struggling with the problem of telling a story about salmon, I read the novella *The Great God Pan* by Arthur Machen. In it, a late Victorian doctor performs psychosurgery on a young woman, forcing her to see past the ordinary and into the divine truth that underlies all reality. It is a terrible truth, perhaps because the woman who sees it had no choice in the matter of her transformation, but was the powerless object of someone else's psychic research. I wonder, though, what would happen to someone who chose to see the other world. We are constantly expanding our sensorium, and our consciousness stretches out into the tools we use, whether they extend our reach or our senses. How must we remake ourselves to perceive not the Great God Pan, but a salmon forest?

Wider than the Sky, Deeper than the Sea

Remy still sometimes itched at the keloid scar where, ten years before, a surgeon had incised the skin of her shoulderblades and installed hundreds of titanium pins wirelessly networked to a tiny computer near the base of her spine. The keloid was tense and shiny, but not large enough to interfere with the action of her arm. Most of her other scars had been more obedient, lying flat, so only with a summer tan could you see the pale scalpel lines drawn across her body.

Each scar was an augmentation, the visible remains of her biggest career achievements. And, really, all she had left of them. For twenty years she had been a leading member of a performance art collective called the Society of Perceptualists, dedicated to extending human perception through technology. Electrodes and loops of wire and tiny transmitters extended her hearing so she heard as a cat did, a rat, a blue whale, a bat. She was attuned to tectonic vibrations with an elephant's seismoperception. She felt the world not through the five or ten senses particular to human evolution, but with a brilliant, disorienting synesthesia that made

---

Author's Note: The performance art described in this story owes a lot to Stelarc and Neil Harbisson. Also, I borrowed the metal tail from one of my brother's BFA projects, as well as a line from "Bushed" by Earle Birney: "a mountain so large his mind slowed when he looked at it" becomes "a woman's mind might slow."

the air pulse and glitter around her, that let her glimpse the electromagnetic spectrum beyond visible light, and sense shifting currents in air and water with her hair follicles. In her twenty years with the Perceptualists, she had received millions in experimental medical interventions, all funded by tech-sector patrons she never met, for whom Eidolon and his Society were pet projects. Those strangers — rich as God — had paid for the iridium filaments that circled her temporal lobe, the platinum and titanium and rhodium that allowed her to hear radio frequencies, Bluetooth. Her umwelt was utterly singular and very very expensive.

Remy did not regret the scars. She didn't even regret the fibroids or the loose skin on her inner forearms and ankles where she had once hosted ears — bat-shaped — made of lab-grown cartilage derived from her rib cage. That skin would never return to its original shape and she had declined plastic surgery to correct the pouches, preferring to preserve the bodily record of her artistic practice. She did not regret the headaches, nor the hyperethesia. Not the psilocybin-enhanced livestreams, the years she'd spent learning to echolocate, to see through her tongue, to hear through the bat-eared implants in her ankles.

Once, she'd hung suspended in the air above the crowd gathered in a flooded Venetian street for the last Biennale the city ever hosted, a season before the storm surge that destroyed the Piazza San Marco. Her body an antenna, attuned to the whole city, her nervous system firing madly to integrate sensation — chemical, vibrational, electromagnetic — human beings had not evolved to perceive.

✦

She left the Perceptualists when she was forty-five. These days she lived alone in a one-room A-frame from the seventies, with wood heat and an almond-colored fridge that leaked and an avocado-green bathtub where — if she remembered to turn on the boiler — she took long baths that eased the ache in her hips and shoulders, a sleep mask over her eyes to get her through the headaches and the constant noise of her aging implants. The cabin stood near a tiny, clear lake in the foothills above the valley, where the interior mountain range ran like a spine down the island's back. Below her cabin ran a small, marginal salmon stream, where for a hundred thousand generations, chinook had been born, had left, and had returned.

She'd retreated to the woods for a project that was supposed to kickstart her post-Perceptualist career. "The Salmon Map" was her working title when she received funding from the Earth Species Project (ESP), The Cetacean Translation Initiative (CETI), and the Canada Council (CC), with a little extra cash from Ducks Unlimited (DU). When she approached them, she still had the Perceptualist's glow around her, so funding was easy. An art star, briefly. The glow hadn't lasted. She'd spent the first checks cleaning up old debt and buying unnecessary equipment, hundreds of tiny cameras, thousands of mics, and enough computing power to handle all the data.

The stream was in decline as temperatures rose and wildfires consumed the hillsides. A hundred thousand generations, and she was watching one of the last cohort of quick, silver fry head out for the deep ocean. That's what she'd pitched in her proposal: a super-sensory act of witness, watching the last chinook carry out their genetically-mandated journey while the world burned down around them. She walked it three or four times a week, daily if she could manage it, though she wasn't as strong as she had once been, and the metal in her body conducted cold right through her skin to her bones. She had never, ever, been as cold as she had been that January, searching a flooded pool for microphones blown away by the rainstorms, her titanium-enhanced fingers too numb to hold a screwdriver.

But now it was September and it hadn't rained since June. Cracks in the clay underfoot, sunrises and sunsets stained orange by wildfire smoke from the mainland. The salmon stream remained cool enough that the yearling fry survived the heatwave, overshadowed by the Douglas fir their parents had fertilized, and which they also would one day feed, when they returned five years heavier from grazing the north Pacific. That is the logic of the salmon forest: the transcontinental, trans-species flow of calories from deep ocean to high forest, calories that traveled in the bodies of salmon, to the mouths of bears and eagles, transfigured in digestive systems and shat out in the deep woods, where they fed the salal and the chanterelle.

"Never underestimate," she had written in her proposal, getting a little lyrical, "the power of shit. Think of our own history: the rivers we have diverted, the infrastructure we've developed to manage our shit. The piles of bear scat studded with salmon bones, maggoty, purple with salal berries. All that is the salmon forest."

And now here she was at the other end of the grants, nothing to show but terabytes of audio data from the stream. Tens of thousands of hours of video from trail cams and drones. A million photographs. Raw, impenetrable numbers recording the water's temperature, acidity, microbial density, and agricultural run-off. She'd caught and tagged a few hundred of the stream's chinook, and the brave, surviving individuals were out of Saanich Inlet and into the north Pacific now, where on maps she saw their slow progress up the Gulf of Alaska toward the Bering Sea. When she arrived, she'd been sure that all the data would capture the true, elusive nature of a salmon forest. It didn't.

Sometimes when she was walking the stream, she saw things in her peripheral vision, artifacts, gleams. When she floated in the shallow lake below her cabin, she heard something in the water. Not a voice. But something. She thought, I can catch those, reproduce them in an installation, send people through a dark corridor full of scent and infrasound, so they could feel the world as a forest would. But even after a year, the perceptions were too elusive for meaning, just the sense of something larger than she could quite name, all around her, and beyond the reach of all her augmentations.

✦

She'd grown up near salmon forests, but she was a city kid, so no field trips to the spawning grounds in October, to gag on the rich stink of rotting fish and startle bald eagles from their hunt. Salmon meant sashimi on a melamine plate at some late-night all-you-can-eat place, or the way her cat purred when she opened a tin of sockeye.

But then maybe ten years ago, the Perceptualists were in Seattle at a small, loud restaurant, after tech rehearsal for the next day's event. Eidolon ordered chuka idako for the table, delicate purple tentacles curled tightly around their bodies, like the infants had contracted in terror as they were executed. She couldn't eat them. Eidolon teasing her, said, "You're eating salmon. How is that different? I'm sure an octopus would eat me if it could."

"Sure. Okay. I just can't." She'd been thinking a lot about octopuses that year, wondering about distributed consciousness, and whether she could build a tentacle to extend from her shoulder. Maybe two. Metal and plastic at first, but cartilage eventually, if she could get Eidolon to give her the resources and lead her own project. A flexible structure alive with filaments jacked into her nervous system. She'd visited a lot of aquariums, watching octopuses glide through the water, and tiptoe over the gravel floors.

She'd even thought one returned her gaze, and she'd rested her head against the glass between them, shutting her eyes and cranking her augmentations so she could listen to the sound of its limbs.

A single tentacle hung from Eidolon's smile. "Fine," he said. "I'll eat yours." And the chopsticks zoomed in to snatch up another baby. She turned to the salmon sashimi and the guy beside her, local tech hired for the event, who'd suggested the place, still serving decent food at two on a Thursday morning.

"You want some?" she asked.

"Naw, man. I worked on a salmon farm one summer and I can't even look at it anymore."

"Oh?" she said, conversational autopilot. Gyroscoping zaps at the back of her brain as she came down from the sensory glories of tech rehearsal, which required her to turn it all up to eleven, testing amps and monitors and screens and feedback loops and her internal EEG. On the other side of the restaurant, someone was eating ice. She could feel the pressure on the stranger's teeth as each cube shattered. On the street outside she had heard the rats creeping through the garbage in the alley and stopped to listen to their tiny sniffles and giggles and the hungry way they chewed.

He was still talking, she realized. "It's the sea lice. Farmed fish are covered in them. It's kind of hard to look at that —" Here he gestured to her glistening sashimi. "— and not think lice. When you think about what they come from, like when they're free, it's —"

He shuddered. She dipped the piece of melon-pink salmon in soy sauce, then pressed it against the roof of her mouth until the flesh split. She chewed. Up above, the fans were turning, and if she let herself, she'd fall into the noise: the faint whir of the motor, and behind that, electricity coursing through the walls, the heartbeat of the man beside her —

She struggled to ask an ordinary human question, like a person, then gave up and ate another piece and marveled at the richness of sound and vision entwined and brilliant and through it all, the taste of salmon.

Maybe that was the moment she started thinking about salmon forests, so her year in this A-frame had its origins while she was still with the Perceptualists, still submerged in Eidolon's vast and visionary ambition, which required years of commitment to design, surgery, recovery, performance, and documentation. There wasn't time to pursue extra octopodal limbs if you were scheduled to have a few thousand hair-thin titanium pins installed in your skeleton and synced to the seismic monitoring network in Hawaii.

◆

She'd begun the Salmon Map in a gloriously windy autumn, the stream in full spate and the rain heavy, the chinook fighting their way up toward pools where golden maple leaves floated. She found chanterelles under the salal bushes and ate them with butter and wondered if she could detect the faint oceanic taste of the salmon carcasses on which they fed. She could not, but she'd read that trees in a salmon forest were so rich in Nitrogen 15 that they had more in common with kelp than with a Douglas fir outside the salmon's dominion.

For weeks, she binged on chanterelles, golden and nutty, foraging as she walked from the cabin to the stream's mouth. Then the season changed and they were gone and she tried to see what was next in the forest's calendar: the scent of rot fading into the sweetness of fallen leaves; at night she no longer heard the lumber of black bears waddling through the undergrowth. The winter season was thick with chilly mist, so at night she dreamed of beautiful equatorial cities, where she had once channeled whole universes of sensation into the tiny, unaugmented minds of the people who came to watch the Perceptualists perform.

On a night in January she heard a woman screaming and started out of bed to unlock the door and stumble onto the porch. But of course it was not a woman, it was a cougar calling out in a voice so human she had to convince herself that a woman did not stand beneath her windows, crying to her for help. The next morning she saw its paw prints in the muddy earth below her front step, dissolving in the rain. Each morning they reappeared. After that she heard the screams of rabbits and had to cover her head with a pillow to stop herself from going outside. Then one night the cougar, sated, moved on. Now she heard the call of owls, a low pulse outside her window, and she added those sensations to the salmon stream's temporal map.

✦

The first words Eidolon ever said to Remy were "Vomeronasal organ."

She was twenty-three. She was unpleasantly sweaty, the nervous kind that probably didn't smell great. She waited for him to elaborate; he did not. They sat in silence and then he began to ask her questions, punctuated by further observations about the Vomeronasal organ, and its absence in the human animal. She talked about building a tail in her undergrad, out of metal strapping she'd pulled from dumpsters at a building site on campus. How it had hung to the ground from her waist, and changed her balance when she ran, and she'd learned that she sensed the ground across which it dragged, its vibrations giving her a picture of the space behind her. He'd nodded. Then he'd described acoustic lenses in the heads of toothed whales, and the way their skulls acted like satellite dishes, focusing infrasound for echolocation. He talked about heat-detecting organs in the noses of snakes, and electrical perception in sharks.

She wasn't sure how that first meeting had gone, but then she was invited for a second and third interview. Because, Eidolon later explained, they needed exactly the right kind of batshit for their Society. She sat in small, silent rooms where the air was curiously dead and her voice did not echo when she spoke. Her hearing tested average. In meetings with psychologists, she related moments of joy, rage, and desire. Having established her emotional excesses and her limited capacity for self-regulation, they tested her enteroception, her proprioception, her ability to perceive her heartbeat, and to keep her balance while blindfolded. Here she excelled. There was an fMRI during a carefully controlled LSD trip that allowed them to map the unregulated corridors of her brain.

The Society's neurologist explained the default mode network, and showed her recordings of her brain, a wrinkled walnut inside her skull, where a significant part of her resided. That connectome is me, she thought, transfixed by the flickering image, or close as I'll ever see.

But not all that she was. With the Perceptualists, she learned that the category of "I" extended beyond her skin. Into the conté she had learned to love as a kid, dragging crayons across paper. Then into the cursor she dragged through virtual landscapes. Into the head of the rivet hammer as she built her tail from metal strapping. Her mind alive to the cutting edge of her knife as she sliced carrots and deboned a chicken thigh. Eidolon explained: you already loop out into the world, along the line of your attention, and into a tool. So why not do the same with tools that extend sensation? All we need are electrical pulses and wire and sensors and our minds can take in the whole world. Beyond the world. Even without a vomeronasal organ.

◆

If she timed it right, she walked from her cabin to low tide along the streambed, following its channel through the mud to the inlet's deep, oceanic stink; on hot days it smelled fecal, especially after the heatwave that killed half the shellfish.

Orcas rolled in the sunlight. They were all waiting for salmon: the seagulls and the eagles, the bears, the chanterelles. All hungry for summer's surfeit, the last feast before the cold, when they could only dream of cracking the salmon skulls and eating their brains. Closer to shore and keeping their distance from the orca, sea lions rafted, and dolphins played in groups of three or four. A couple of boys in a boat were drifting in the slack September water, also waiting for the returning chinook.

Somewhere far down Saanich inlet, the first salmon made their way through this gauntlet. They'd arrive to be fished from the water by spears and paws and nets, and if they survived that, they'd tear their bellies on the creek's stones, their bodies a single, tense muscle flipping them out of the water and over the obstacles. The chinook were drawn irresistibly homeward from the deep ocean where they fed from creatures rising from Okhotsk and the bottom of the Bering Sea. She was ankle deep in a path that ran a quarter of the way around the globe.

The adults stopped eating once they crossed from saltwater to fresh. They might live for a day after their terminal creative act, drifting above their eggs. She wondered what their last thoughts were. Were they briefly conscious of being unhitched from the imperatives that drove them downstream in the first place. If she could ask a salmon — or a salmon forest — anything, it would be about the last hours of their lives.

◆

For her entire history with the Perceptualists, Eidolon was silent about his plans, preferring to talk over immediate problems: how many underskin hooks it took to support a 75.3 kilogram adult male body over the Las Vegas strip; whether it was legal to be naked and suspended above the Las Vegas strip. He'd talk about painkillers and new work from the Earth Species Project, where they recorded whalesong and tracked the pheromonal shimmer of ant colonies, hoping to recognize linguistic patterns in other animals. But that was chit-chat. He only ever told her what he wanted when he was sure. Then she'd see the diagrams, the surgical plan, and imagine how her forearms and ankles were to be transfigured into ears.

Once they sat together in his garden, she was dumb with oxy after a thousand pins had been implanted in her bones. He — dreamy, pinprick pupils — told her that when he was ten his father bought him this cybernetic conversion kit for cockroaches. He'd caught a roach and clipped its antennae and superglued the battery to its back, then he'd sat with his phone, a twelve-year-old boy and also a god, directing the roach in circles around a plastic ice cream bucket until he got tired, and put the lid on.

But inside the ice cream bucket, the roach was still attuned to the electrical pulses of the battery, and ran in exhausted circles. When he returned the next day, it was dead.

"It all began there," he said. "All of it."

He was more careful with the next cockroach, 3D printed a backpack to support a larger battery, superglued it to the insect's carapace. It ran circles as he nudged antennae and the cerci at its rear, its legs skittering each time he tapped his phone. It died content, well-fed, on a weekend he was away at his Dad's place. The next day, he removed the backpack and started again.

"Poor cockroach," she said.

"Yes. I did feed him bacon, though. He liked that. I fed them all bacon, and some of them lived, oh, weeks with those little batteries on their backs. I learned so much from them. I'm grateful."

She wondered how they understood the imperatives that had them running circles around the ice cream buckets. Did they think it was god? An evil spirit? Did the cockroaches ever get to stop and lick the remaining drips of sugary vanilla from the corners? Eidolon probably scrubbed them clean. He was scrupulous. He had to be with all those hooks under his skin.

The cockroach circled behind her eyes and she was suddenly exhausted, aching, still hungover from the general anaesthetic, with the Vicodin and cortisol and adrenaline and Ger's injections. "It's B12," he always told her, tight-lipped. "Don't worry, it's organic."

But Eidolon always handled recovery better than she did. In the other lounge chair, he was still talking: "People who've lost their visual cortex but still have the optic tectum will believe themselves blind, but nevertheless still process visual information. I wonder, sometimes, if there are other organs of perception we do not consciously register, but which tell us about the world. Do you know l'appel du vide?"

She shook her head, the cockroach ran circles and circles.

"I sometimes think that l'appel du vide is that calling to us, saying come here, come here." She shuddered. Maybe that was how the cockroach felt his jabs at the smartphone screen: the irresistible call, l'appel du vide.

✦

Her skeleton was full of tiny pins because of one of Eidolon's plans. He'd come to her and said, "I have an idea." Those four words had changed her life at least a dozen times before, but this would be the last time. They were in his garden. She waited and he pulled out his tablet. "Can you imagine what it feels like to be a tectonic plate?"

She could imagine what it was like to be most mammals, many birds, one mollusk (an octopus). But thinking of fault lines and centuries of tension building up — it made her jaw clench. "What are you thinking?" she asked.

"Osseointegrated pins. Femur, tibia, scapula, pelvis. And then this." He offered her a handful of colored wires, coiled around a tiny device. "In your anterior precuneus. It's a prototype."

"Okay, but," she said, right hand wandering to the tissue expander in her left fore-arm. "We have networked pins and we have the electrode, but what does it do?"

He giggled the way he did when he was really excited, a nervous little boy's giggle, like he couldn't believe he was getting away with it. Then the new diagrams, not of a brain, but of the Pacific Ocean.

"Seismic monitoring station," he said, jabbing at the screen until they zoomed into a dot on the map. "When you're synced to the station, you'll feel what it's like to be a planet."

"Seismoperception," she said, thinking of the way elephants communicate through the ground, sensing patterned stomps from their herd ten kilometers away. Her arm was still in a sling from the last procedure, which had installed the tissue-expanders in her forearms, to make room for bat ears. The ears were being built in the lab right now, nurtured on the backs of rats. She had been able to imagine that, echolocation and the thin, high spectrum of bat perception. But this —

She picked up the device and imagined a thousand hair-thin pins in her bones, triggered by an earthquake and rumbling.

"So you're synced to the station, and an earthquake will trip the anterior precuneus electrode. Instant disembodiment, floating like you're on ketamine or ether. Separated from the lizard brain bullshit and out somewhere else. It almost makes you believe in a soul," he said, dreamy. "But at the same time, perceiving tectonic action. Amazing, huh?"

She had managed other things: infra- and ultra-sound, sensory substitution using her tongue, to perceive ultraviolet light; with the tips of her fingers she'd learned to perceive electrical currents the way a shark did. But this was more: her whole skeleton attuned to tectonic stimulus.

"How do we document?"

"The EEG you've already got. Some film of your skin. Hyperethesia analog for the compression waves of an earthquake. It'll be spectacular."

She shuddered.

"Yeah, like that," he said, watching her critically. "That could be interesting."

"It's kind of like a spider," she said as she grasped what he had imagined. "In a web. Distributed consciousness along all the lines of silk. But instead of a web, we have a seismograph's sensors. And instead of mechanoreceptive hairs, I have a couple of thousand titanium pins. But otherwise, it's kind of the same?"

◆

Today, in the salmon forest, the pins were still in her bones, and because she couldn't afford to have them extracted, they were still activated by the lowest frequencies around her. That could be the earth or water or maybe radio waves, human or interstellar. Synthetic stereocilia, transducing vibration and bone conduction integrated this new sense that was not, exactly, sound.

The electrode that Eidolon showed her was part of a system designed for Parkinson's patients, with secondary uses for severe OCD and resistant depression, a subtle and effective form of electroshock therapy. You had to crack the system to make it do what they needed, give her the jolt of disembodiment, smash the brain/body/soul barrier. It was what you'd call an "off label" use, like the electrode she knew Eidolon had implanted in his nucleus accumbens, which hadn't been designed to produce perfect joy by way of a twenty-thousand dollar battery. Ecstasy, when he cranked it.

Eventually, the rumble of titanium pins would become second nature to her, Eidolon insisted. It might hurt sometimes — the hooks hurt, after all — but she'd adjust.

But then, when she was still recovering from surgery and experimenting with new sensations, someone, somewhere, opened the floodgates to a seismograph during a 6.3 magnitude 30km below the surface, and she'd synced to the shock wave, undifferentiated sensation overspilled the titanium pin system, triggering a cascade that lit up every implant, her entire nervous system spiking sound and color, a violent and obliterating synesthesia. She couldn't tell what was her and what was the grinding Pacific plate and that was bad enough, but a crescendo tripped the implant in her anterior precuneus and she left her body, suddenly hovering a meter, then two, then ten, above it. Until she was through the roof and out in a darkness suffused with reverberations and echoes. She was a string resonating to a distant sound, a bell ringing in sympathy, no longer herself. Not anyone anymore.

She woke up fourteen hours later in the clinic with Ger nearby, muttering over her blood pressure. Her body still sputtering with sensation so oppressive she could not distinguish sight from sound from taste. She wanted to speak but she'd probably just groaned, something primal, infantile, that said only *help me help me.*

But she recovered, right? So why did she lose her nerve? For the first time in her decades with the Perceptualists, she was afraid that she had reached the limits of her body, and that beyond lay obliteration, crossed wires and synaptic feedback loops that would shatter any sense of self she had left.

Eidolon knew. When she tried to talk to him, his eyes were blank and distant, his skin shivering with hyperethesia, like a dreaming cat's. No one knew what had triggered those waves across his skin, only that one could watch him respond to unknown stimuli.

When she recovered enough to ask Ger, he shook his head. "Who even knows what he's reacting to. So many sensors and only so much neurological real estate. I'm surprised he can still taste anything, or walk. I'm surprised he can still draw."

✦

By late August, at the end of her year in the salmon forest, she avoided her email because it was full of messages from Project CETI about her data, and a Gentle Reminder from the Canada Council that her final report was due in six weeks. An interview request for the Earth Species Project website. But then she missed a rare message from Eidolon, just a link to a comped ticket for a Perceptualist event at some magnificent performance space in San Francisco. A single word: coming?

She shouldn't go. Couldn't afford it. The reports were due.

Before she left the forest, she dialed everything down so she wouldn't be obliterated by crowds and airplane engines and the cries of rats in alleyways. It was miserable, like the world had gone dimensionless and how could anyone stand being that way?

Unable to hear the capillary action in trees, or the heartbeats of the people sitting nearby. She couldn't stand it, so she turned them back up and was swamped by the vibrations of SFO and then the city's streets, rendering her almost speechless after months in the woods.

She arrived at the venue when the doors opened, like an ordinary person. Waited an hour, nervous. Behind locked doors, or underground in offices and rehearsal spaces, the Perceptualists were preparing the evening's event, the last-minute disasters and scrambles.

And then there was Eidolon: a small, naked man on a plinth, sliding hundreds of hooks under his skin, then lifted ten meters overhead. She walked around the room's perimeter, listening at each confluence of speakers, listening to the low susurrations of the crowd fed back to them, remixed by sound engineers in an office somewhere, responding in real time to the audio from Lux's implants. Their enhanced vision, heat sensing, infrared, ultraviolet translated into images that thrummed with otherwise-invisible life. Up above, sunset broke through the atrium's enormous glass walls, and the room was flooded with light.

An hour later, she was going to leave with the crowd because what was the point of lingering, looking needy and lonely. But she was reading artists' statements near the main doors when an absurdly young tech stopped her.

"You're Remy? There's an after-party."

Through a locked door, to a large and brilliant room where Eidolon stood, twenty years further along the path of augmentation than she was. He had to be nearly seventy. The left side of his face drooped. She'd heard he'd designed a cluster of electromagnetic sensors to circle the orbit of his left eye, and integrate with his optic nerve and his tongue. It would double his field of vision.

"Distributed consciousness," he was saying as she joined the edge of the circle around him, his speech muffled. His eyes flicked once to her, then he carried on. "I was watching the spiders in my garden. New implants, sure, so I can operate, but the sensory inputs aren't that different than they would be for a spider — just the silk tugging away at me through the hooks in my skin. Remy."

Then the conversation wasn't general. He limped through the admirers to put his arms around her.

"Do those hurt? Or did you crank your nucleus accumbens? I saw some artifacts — like in your peripheral vision —" He leaned toward her, inclining his good right ear, but she realized he couldn't understand what she said. Around them young artists were hovering, hoping to be noticed. The noise seemed to drag his eyes from place to place, then he shaded his eyes with his hand and she understood.

"I need a drink. Do you need a drink?" she shouted.

He heard that. Nodded. Together they made their way through the watching crowd to a quieter bar in the atrium over-looking the water, where a young woman in black poured her two glasses of beer.

At the bottom of the beer, Eidolon seemed to recollect himself.

"It tastes terrible," he said.

She waited for him to say more.

"Dysgeusia. The implants. Everything tastes terrible now."

She nodded. "What else are you working on?"

"Besides this old circus act? Investors still like the hooks. The blood."

A brief pause, and then it was like time hadn't passed at all: they were back where they had been for twenty years, chewing through technical problems and audience perception, blue-skying and troubleshooting. The dead-ends, and half-ideas they could not yet pursue, the limits against which they struggled. Eidolon talked about the spiderweb, and the scars of his most recent surgeries. The bruising had been bad, he said. And he still wasn't happy with the left side, especially the weakness in his shoulder. But why should only perfection be considered success?

Then it was her turn. She launched into what she was looking for: the umwelt not of a single species, but of a trans-Pacific flow of energy. Bodies. Nutrients. How the money was running out. How the ESP grant officer sent her eager messages she hadn't yet answered, and Project CETI wanted all the audio she'd collected from the dolphins and pilot whales and orca hovering near the mouth of the stream.

Eidolon was silent for so long that she began to worry. She was about to stand and signal the young woman behind the bar when Eidolon's eyes shifted, and he shut his mouth, sucking the bead of saliva back between his lips.

"You have," he said, "within your mind a map of your body, and not only that — a map of what your body perceives around you. A neurological topography that reflects the world's shape, in whatever mode you grasp it — sound or vision or scent. You recreate inside what you perceive outside, just as you create a homunculus within your brain, the neurological model of your body. You can perceive — and process — sensation far beyond the grasp of our conscious mind."

As he always had, Eidolon grasped what really mattered in the morass of her ideas.

"The last generation of Chinook. It is glorious," he said. His eyes glazed, the lids half-closed, and that bead of drool re-formed on his lip. Like he was hearing something beyond even her capacities. "I've seen the pictures," he added. "Wildfires."

"They're getting closer," she said. "The sunlight is pink and orange all day, like in a movie musical. The sky reminds me of clay. Like. Biscuit."

He spoke slowly, deliberately, each word a struggle against the slack muscles around his mouth. "If it's not working, it's not working. Maybe it's time to come home."

That stopped her because she'd always thought leaving the Perceptualists was a one-way door.

"You could bring your data home. I'm sure we could do something to satisfy the stakeholders. Get something into a gallery. And then you could come back to work."

She imagined leaving the A-frame and the forest and the wildfire sunrises, the sound of the bears lumbering through the woods.

"What are you planning?" she asked.

He seemed limp now, struggling to say, "Tianyan."

She understood: the Pacific Earthquake project — the one sunk in her own bones — was just one step toward Eidolon's ultimate goal, which wasn't to process tectonic vibrations, but something much larger. Tianyan in Guizhou. Heaven's eye. The largest radio telescope array in the world.

"But seismoperception nearly killed me — is a radio telescope even possible?"

He grunted, incredulous. "I want to hear the universe calling to me. I want to look back at heaven. How can you not? Electromagnetic pulses from the very origin of the universe. Background radiation and exploding stars and light and the emanations of black holes. How can you not want to hear what the universe has to say?"

He was turning away from her then. Back to the crowd and the noise, and all the people who wanted to touch him, to ask him a question, tell him how inspiring he was. She said, "Eidolon —"

He shook his head. "If you want to come with me, you should. Otherwise —"

"I could have died. You could die."

"But you didn't. And you know that one body isn't enough. It's not even enough for your salmon forest. That's why you haven't produced anything." He leaned forward onto one hand, the other shading his peripheral vision. "You do realize it's not working, don't you? I can hear it in your voice."

She was surprised by how much that hurt.

"I know what's calling me, Remy. What's calling you? If you can answer that, you might actually have something with your salmon. If you can't —" He shrugged. "Come with me instead."

He tried to stand and failed. She touched his slack left arm. "Do you need help?"

"Maybe." Terse now. "Doctors are getting all." Here he waved his hand, dismissive. "I'm fine. You seem fine. There are new technologies — I can't even explain them to you. We could be Heaven's Eye. We'll be able to sync across the augmentations and Tianyan. The neurological processing power of two bodies and a massive radio telescope. Can you imagine it? The deepest, most ancient parts of the universe."

He was saying "we" but behind it she heard what she had always heard from Eidolon: I.

"And I can tell — they're wearing, aren't they? The electrode in your nucleus — can you afford to do maintenance? We'll look after all of that, of course."

It surprised her that he knew. She couldn't even afford to have them removed until the problems were acute enough to be covered by provincial health, and as it was, her GP looked sideways at her when she visited, limping, blinded by headaches. What were you thinking, the woman's eyes seemed to ask. How could it possibly have been worth it?

"Think about it," he said.

◆

Back at the A-frame, she spent three days in bed listening to this brown noise mix she'd started when she arrived the year before. It was months of forest audio and her own heartbeats layered into a 48 hour track, high frequencies cut until it formed a kind of warm static. When she woke in the night to that rumble, she thought, hazily, that this was what it would sound like to be in utero, all bloodflow and heartbeat, the rhythm of a huge metabolism. On bad days she often lay on the floor and let the sound of the salmon forest overwash her, tracking the artifacts in her vision, the glimmer in her peripheral, that might mean anything. A salmon forest is an entity so huge, a woman's mind might slow when she tries to approach it.

Sometimes when she woke in the night, she felt the earth breathing. She called it sound, but that was only shorthand for what suffused her bones when underwater sensors transmitted the bottom end of the spectrum past her skin and into her body.

The next day she woke up in the wildfire dawn and felt strong enough to swim in the lake, the water too warm for September. As she drifted, she felt herself lifted, disembodied, losing cohesion in the salmon forest, and she heard the yearling fry along the gravel beds up and down the creek. And if she leaned into that bodiless-ness, she reached beyond the stream, beyond the inlet and the channel and into the north Pacific, and she reached into the roots of trees, and the guts of seagulls, too. The lumbering bear, the hunting cat.

She started and maybe that triggered it, because she felt something like ether or ketamine, and she was yanked out of her body and now floated a few meters above the salmon stream's headwaters. Here in the trees, where she could sense something moving. Below her, the stream spilled from the lake, and looking down through the water she saw the glint of yearling fry among the green-tinted gravel.

There it is, she thought, reaching for the forest in the moment that it evaporated and she returned to her body.

✦

She walked back to the A-frame and called Eidolon, relieved when it went to voicemail and she could stutter out the truth: *no I can't go back to that.*

Eidolon never spoke to her again.

But she still imagined him. Or maybe it wasn't imagination — maybe some part of her looped out across the world toward him, the way it looped into the stream. After she left her terminal message, she walked down to the lake to float and listen for the chinook. She closed her eyes and sank into sensation and could — if she dreamed hard — imagine where he was. Her vision was so clear, she wondered if she had slid into some lucid dream, where she occupied his body. She could feel the weakness on his left side, the pain of fourteen hours' travel in his left shoulder, his arm curled protectively around his ribs. How hard it was to drink water, though Ger constantly fussed at him to stay hydrated. The rain was falling. His shirt stuck to him, and he wanted to get something out of his bag, but his left hand was too weak, so he snapped at Ger — come on, come on. Drool on his chin again. But all worth it because Heaven's Eye was waiting for him.

Now Eidolon lay on a gurney, Ger hovering. She should be with him now, their brainwaves entrained, waiting for a burst of particles from the origins of the universe to shuttle through the telescope and the telescope to transduce those electrons into something his body could sense.

On the other side of the Pacific, Eidolon felt a low rumble in his bones. Oscillations so tiny he had to close his eyes to observe them, like a faint and distant earthquake, the nearly undetectable vibration that reminds you that you are part of the planet.

Far above him, the atmosphere shivered. But he wasn't on the planet anymore, not really. He was the planet, the electromagnetic pulses of deep space careening off the surface of the atmosphere, the magnetic field, and if he concentrated, he'd hear through the interference into something far beyond it. His body an exposed nerve. His body an ear, listening.

When she woke she was sure it had been a dream, but there was a message from Ger. *It's not going well. Watch out for that electrode in your precuneus, Rem. Get it out if you can. Or at least turn it off. Turn them all off if you want a shot at living much longer. Will let you know when he wakes up.*

That morning, she walked to the stream's mouth, the fallen cedar tree with its mussel-covered branches. A chinook struggled toward fresh water and she thought of the boulders and stumps in its way and she felt nothing but a kind of exhausted sympathy.

First, she thought. My right ankle —

✦

Fifteen years before, she'd left through the back door of an absurdly expensive restaurant in Manhattan where, long after closing, Eidolon held court with investors and journalists. She'd stood alone in the alley, so still that the rats in the garbage had re-emerged. With the implant in her right ankle, she'd listened to them skitter and chew and climb, their busy night's work punctuated by squeaks and giggles inaudible to ordinary human ears. That weekend she'd walked twenty km of back alleys recording the city's invisible wilderness. She'd hunted for the tiny sounds that mice made in walls, the crinkle of cockroaches and the snap-crackle-pop maggots make in bags of trash and dead bodies. Back home, she'd dropped those ultrasonic squeaks and scratches into the top of the human range and laughed to listen to the secret world of the garbage can.

Eidolon had hated it. "Repulsive," he said. "We want sublimity, not rot." She'd loved the track, had dreamed of whole installations grounded in the world of the rat and the cockroach. But nothing had ever come of it.

✦

Her left ankle. The underwater noises faded to nothing but a few misfires in her auditory cortex before that settled into — not silence, but a limited little umwelt. How foolish it was to be human, rather than rat or blue whale. You heard such a tiny sliver of the world.

Only in their absence did she realize she'd been listening to the off-shore conversations of dolphins, the flick of chinooks' tails against gravel upstream. The interplay of waves from a billion sources and moments up and down the inlet, the north Pacific, the whole of the world's reverberating oceans. Beneath those regular animal conversations, she had sensed the rhythm of shelled creatures, the flick of barnacle cilia filtering microorganisms and marine snow from the rich green waters. The voice of a living ocean.

Gone. Then the sensors around her ears, that circled the back of her skull. The forest behind her fell silent.

◆

Once, a decade before, she had sat with a bamboo plant for an afternoon, and had insisted to Eidolon that those tiny ripples you could see in her EEG recording? That was the sound of a plant reaching up into the sunshine, transforming light into sugar.

◆

The sound of water rising through the capillaries of Douglas fir had been her constant unacknowledged companion for months. But now the richest and strangest parts of the world had fled from her, hiding in the flat light of the every day. She wanted them back, all the tiny vibrations of the salmon forest, not this sad, hollow wreck of a body. It was lonely to hear the voices of dolphins fall silent, but to know they still chattered.

It was like the moment you leave a concert and are out the hall's back door and into a side street and it's so quiet, you feel disoriented until your ears awaken to the night-sounds of the city and the people around you. Or maybe like you're thirteen and your favorite song is over after the fifth replay and you stop dancing in your bedroom and just stand there, wondering what happens next. Silence so empty it made her long to crank them all back up and let whatever was going to happen, happen.

◆

On the other side of the Pacific, Eidolon felt the universe open wide, pour into his tiny human brain. Or maybe he didn't. Maybe that was all her imagination, and Eidolon was knocked unconscious by sensations that were impossible to integrate or understand. Maybe when she imagined him, it was all a sympathetic invention, like voices in the undergrowth, and the chatter of salal, and the slow conversations that trees have across the centuries.

◆

It was twilight. She could hear people from the other side of the stream, where a few rusted iron barbecues stood in the concrete beside picnic tables. A kid was laughing. Girls were singing along with the thin bleed of a phone speaker. She waded across the stream, then crunched over the shingle to the park, and the smell of salmon barbecue. Picnic tables covered with juice bottles and salad bowls, children thieving pre-dinner potato chips. Now Grandma's admonishing voice saying wait, don't fill up on junk. She was staring at them, she knew, but it was because she wanted to tell them what she had lost — how out in the inlet the dolphins were in intimate conversation, and how that salmon blood glutted the filter-feeders on the floor of the bay. How the sea lions, bellies full, avoided the inlet's deep, anoxic waters and remained in the sunlit shallows. How on the other side of the horizon the forest had its eastern edge, so distant she could not hear it, not sense it, only knew its limit must be somewhere in the far northern Pacific, where krill hatched 3000m below the surface, feeding on plankton that circulated —

"— Hey," someone said. "You okay?"

It took her a moment to understand the human words, then to think of what "okay" meant and then determine whether the hollow way she felt was "okay." A woman was looking at her, forty-something like Remy. They might have gone to high school together. Concern. That was concern in her voice.

"I think so," Remy said, finally. "I mean, sure I'm okay."

"You're the artist," the woman went on, as though Remy might be the only one. She wondered how long this had been her designation. Oh, it's just the Artist, people said, when they heard her fumbling through the night-time forest, echolocating and soaked to the skin, in search of the salmon's secrets. When she sat for hours on the fallen cedar log on the beach, listening to the conversation of water bugs and chickadees. When they found her trailcams and microphones in the woods, and shook their heads in amusement at the whole ridiculous endeavor. The artist.

The woman continued gently: "We actually met when you did a talk at the library. Last year. How's it going?"

Remy nodded. She couldn't remember the talk at all. Damn.

"I came to dinner afterward," the woman went on. "We were supposed to have coffee at some point, but you know." The woman, as though she knew she was dealing with someone out of her mind, said, "You want to come eat? First chinook of the season. We caught it this afternoon."

Remy discovered she was starving. She relied on a hazy memory of good manners to answer.

"That's really kind of you. If you've got room, I'd love to," she finally said. "Thank you."

Story Notes

I put this story last because it defines my goals for the collection: it is a story about possibility and transformation, even in pain. I wrote it when I was pregnant and scared and thinking about all the other people struggling to bring new life into a dangerous world.

I often feel that the future has been foreclosed upon, and that our culture tells us daily that change is impossible. I know this isn't true, but the belief is insidious. If there's anything I can offer to you, my reader, it is here, as I remind both you and myself that we are protean and contain the possibility of unimaginable transformations. The world has been different before and it will be different again. Maybe even better.

Conclusion: An Incomplete Catalogue of Miraculous Births, or, Secrets of the Uterus Abscondita

Mary Toft, First Part

Mary Toft is in the garden on an August morning rich with bees. Five months along, her belly presses against the rough linen of her skirt while one hand curves protectively around it, half support, half caress. She thinks: this time next year, what will she be? And after that? In the corner of her eye she glimpses a child — like a ghost, or a prefigure — running through the morning from the kitchen door to the garden wall.

She makes her way toward a field the mowers cut three days before. On the way she meets Margaret and together they walk to their day's labor. The mowers are already at work, crossing another field with the regular sweep of their scythes, the second load of the season. Mary and Margaret row the hay already cut and left flat to dry.

It is Mary who disturbs the rabbit, with no ill-intention. An hour earlier the doe had fled the mowers, her heart wild and her eyes rolling white, and hidden among the fallen grass of the field now being rowed. Her breast and her tail are brightly white, and it's the whiteness that stops Mary, as much as the movement, so she is first to look up and see the creature break for the edge of the field, speeding through the stubble and the brittle grass, her rear legs sliding from side to side in fear.

Mary watches the rabbit leap for the ditch. She cannot see it, but she knows — how does she know? — the rabbit stops, listening for those terrors above who would hunt her to earth, who would tear her to pieces and eat her, dragging her heart and stomach out through a rent in her belly. The other women return to their work, but Mary watches, and finds her mind returned to an earlier afternoon, some autumn when she was a child and her father brought home the bloody carcasses of three rabbits, their eyes blank in their sockets, and their paws limp. Mary watched her mother dismantle their bodies, and consign them to the pot, their bones enriching a sauce of thyme and rosemary, their blood and livers added at the end to thicken. She remembered the slender and furless paws, the tiny feet, the delicate ivory bones broken in the dish, the sharp edge where her father's knife, her mother's cleaver, had split the powerful thigh bone, or shattered the ribs. How, taking a mouthful of the stew, she had also taken a mouthful of bone, and the points had scratched inside her cheek.

She can taste rabbit on her tongue, the fear and ferrous of its blood, or perhaps that is the taste of her own, where the bones pierced her cheek. She knows the rabbit still hides — white eyed — in the ditch.

At that moment the child leaps like a rabbit in her womb. She returns to work, one hand often caressing her belly.

That night her labor begins, and what emerges is not a human child, not exactly. It is unsexed, its eyes sealed, its skin dark grey, like a hairless rabbit kitten, with an open pocket that runs from breastbone to privates, and its lungs and liver hanging outside its body.

In the light of a guttering taper it seems to Mary that the child draws one breath, but perhaps it does not. Perhaps his singular moment on earth was — like the morning's prefigure — only a dream.

The Egg From Whence Hatched the World

In the beginning there was only water, and then the egg. The egg might be, for example, the product of a dove descending on the deep. From the egg might hatch a number of different entities, depending on the context. The universe itself might float from that original albumen. Or it might be a man, creeping from the shell on which a raven knocks to waken him. Or no creature at all might escape the cosmic egg, but rather the substance of reality itself, called by some ylem: the original material, the primeval atom.

In at least one instance it was Gaea who crept out of the world-egg, who conceived — with the aid of the waters — her son-lover Ouranos, with whom she populated the world.

The Monstrous Egg, First Part

New Mexico and the Trinity Test Site. In July, a young man climbs a thirty-meter ladder to where the Gadget, armed, awaits its early-morning detonation. He has been assigned babysitting duties in case of sabotage, though he is not sure what he is meant to do if anyone tries to approach his tower. The summer night seems to have arranged its own defense, anyway, and a storm blows in all thunder-struck, lightning-hatched. He spends the night alone, reading by the light of his TL-122-A, the dull yellow center of its beam illuminating half a page at a time, first one comic book then another, until — long before dawn — its narrow circle dims. After that it is only in sudden lightning strikes he sees the whole page at once: the Human Torch, Captain America, Superman defeating fascists. All back-issues he'd picked up in the commissary.

Outside in the darkness and storm — so dark he cannot see the ground, only the wild and disordered air — the Gadget broods; it seems to him, gravid and still, except when a high wind causes the whole tower to groan and sway and another handful of rain drenches the window, its drops caught in freeze-frame flash by lightning.

He is excruciatingly aware of the Gadget, and what lies within it, what chain reactions, what potential. It might be an entirely new world. Or an end to the old world. Or nothing at all, an empty egg, unviable despite their best intentions.

Mary Toft, Second Part

Mary buried the inside-out child. Once, she looked up from its little grave to see rabbits watching in the first rain of September, a flicker of drops across a bright sunset in a slate-colored sky. Her glance scattered the rabbits and they peeled away from the gravesite where she had set a little bunch of cottage flowers — clove pinks, richly scented, from the warm corner beside the front door.

She thought of rabbit stew, and early morning rabbits startled among the lettuces of her little garden. She thought of their white bellies flickering, as had flickered the belly of that rabbit who fled the mowers and haymakers, who had — in a flash of light — quickened within her. She thought: perhaps the womb is transparent, like water, and perhaps the flash of light from a rabbit's white stomach can quicken within, as the word of God quickened in Mary's own womb.

She felt something move, a creature she could not name, and who knows what shape it took? From a smear of blood to a cluster of bones, from a frog to a hairless rabbit kit, to a monkey to a man, to the shape made by certain underground roots who scream when they are torn from the earth. Something moved in that internal darkness, enclosed by the shell of her belly.

The second pregnancy was easier than the first, and the tiny, flickering creature moved within her wild and skittish, so she wondered if she had not one, but a litter of kits inside.

The Prophetess Hen

In August of 1819, in a village outside of Manchester, a farmer announces the advent of a miraculous hen. She lays eggs of remarkable beauty that bear — in copperplate letters — words of hope and advantage: Love your Savior, says one egg. Fear God, says another. Hellfire Awaits.

The hen dies suddenly. The village doctor preserves the remaining eggs. It was not until 1837 that the Farmer — on his deathbed — admits what many suspected: that he had written those messages on newly-lain eggs. When the ink dried he re-inserted them into the hen — well, into multiple hens, but the Prophetess of Manchester was the only one who survived the process more than twice — and waited for the mystery to reveal itself in his chicken coop.

Gaea And Ouranos

Together Gaea and Ouranos conceived Briareos, Kottos, and Gyes, lovely and powerful creatures with fifty heads and fifty arms each. While Gaea loved them for their strength and beauty, Ouranos was troubled by their perfection — their enormous shoulders, their great height, their hundred exquisite eyes. Rather than allowing their power to challenge his own, he pushed them back inside Gaea, who was also the earth, locking them in the underground of Tartarus, which was also Gaea's womb.

Gaea, she cried out in pain, as her sons dragged their fifty arms against the interior of her womb, which was also the deep region beneath the earth. She felt them return, also, to an earlier posture, since Ouranos's violence twisted them into fetal creatures, their fifty arms wrapped around their bodies and their knees drawn up to meet the foreheads of their fifty heads. She felt each kick they made in defiance of her stony womb, each flip and turn as they sought some comfort in the tiny space their father had allowed them. She wept at both the pain and the perversion, and whispered to them: you will live in the air again; you will grow into your final form and you will be free.

Gaea and Ouranos continued to conceive children, and — once born — Ouranos returned them to their mother, until her whole body was occupied, womb and bowels, with creatures waiting to be reborn. With each child her body grew larger, the shell of her belly harder and she could not move with the weight of them.

She would burst, she thought, she would rupture, and all her children would run back out into the world again through her torn navel.

Where Children Thus Are Born With Hairy Coats Heaven's Wrath Unto the Kingdom It Denotes

Monstrous births are prefigures.

In Towton, Yorkshire, in 1461 a child was born hairy from crown to foot, with a head made entirely of barking dogs. The child rose from the bloody sheets in which his mother lay, said fear the flames! and expired. The dogs that constituted his head barked and whimpered a moment longer, then they, too, were still.

The obvious question is: what horror filled his mother's eye or ear or mouth when he — enwombed — was still in flux, a protean creature awaiting his final form? The child's shape is, of course, uncertain until the moment of birth, vulnerable to any number of outside forces. A vision of rabbits. A moment of insight. An internment camp. A refugee trail. A fat man or a little boy. A cigarette. A miraculous gadget. A sudden fright. A new passion. The presence of a beautiful man. The taste of honey. The uninvited touch of a stranger while one is walking through the grocery store minding one's own business. The evil eye. The epigenetic triggers of famine and warzone. Fallout and trace mercury.

Elizabeth Johnson observed the First Battle of Bull Run with her sister, unaware that she had just conceived a child with her now-absent husband, a Confederate officer. Captain Johnson died in the battle, and while she did not observe his death by shrapnel, she did watch a man beheaded by a cannonball. Nothing might have come of it, had he not looked up the hillside in the moment of his decapitation, to where Elizabeth and her sister stood watching.

Should we wonder, then, that Elizabeth gave birth to a headless child in 1862? He lived for three years, and though his body grew, he was never physically competent, could neither walk nor crawl, and made only a whistling, mewling noise. Elizabeth remained a devoted mother to the end, dripping spoon after spoon of warm cream into the gaping sphincter of her son's neck.

Mary Toft, Third Part

Dr. Graves, the man-midwife who attended the birth and death of Mary's inside-out rabbit-child, wrote an account of the new sort of creature that scratched its way from her womb, part man, part Leporidae.

Dr. Graves did not subscribe to the old discourse of marvels and prefigures. He was a rational man, interested in the science of birth, particularly maternal impression, and not the mythology. He was pleased that a mystery had fallen in his lap, and he observed Mary's symptoms with care, nodding sagely when he felt the fever on her brow and ignoring her rambling talk about the flash of a rabbit's belly in the August morning, and the shadow of a little girl running to the bottom of the garden.

"Yes, yes, my dear, now you must rest," he said. Her urgency did not trouble him.

The next day Daniel Toft sent word by way of his sister, Margaret, that Mary was again in labor. Dr. Graves arrived in time to see the aftereffects: the blood soaked sheets, the fragments of pearly bone and tooth. The creature expelled was like the others, but more clearly a rabbit now, as though some progress had been made since she birthed its litter-mates. Dr. Graves took it away and sketched it: its delicate legs, the short ears, the tiny padless paws. If it was not for the blood, its belly would have been white. Not hairless like the earlier kits, this creature was small, but its eyes were open, its claws splayed and bloody in death.

Such well-developed claws must have scratched, he thought, on leaving the maternal seat. He could not determine how it died, but was not surprised at the death of a creature so unsuited to either human or natural worlds.

Dr. Graves combined his account of the birth, his sketches of the rabbit-child of Mary and Daniel Toft, his conjecture on the nature of maternal impressions, and sent them to an acquaintance at the Royal Society. He was gratified to receive a response within the week, an invitation to bring the Tofts to London for observation. Mary's belly was swollen with her seemingly unending pregnancy, and she often talked of her desire for rabbit stew, of rabbits she often saw now, in dreams, fleeing from her, their white bellies flashing. When Dr. Graves examined her, a thick stench emerged from her womb, and there seemed, under the skin, some angry red distemper that spread down her thighs and up toward her navel. Her skin was hot to the touch, and she never seemed to sleep, only to lapse into unconsciousness.

The trip to London was painful for everyone. Mary gave birth to two rabbits on the road, attended by her husband. They sent these children back home with Margaret Toft, Daniel's sister, to be buried with their siblings.

Mary did not know where she was, even when they told her "London." She stayed in dark, closed rooms, refusing light as though it might pierce her, and when the blade of the sun did penetrate her darkness, she shrieked, so that Dr. Graves relented, and examined her by the near-darkness of a candle. He touched her belly, and saw the torn skin of her secret parts, scratched as by claws, or broken bones, as though the creatures had not been born in a gush of blood, but had been dragged by rear foot from the womb, leaving the route of their egress written on her purpled flesh.

Mary was not often conscious. Her fever was often high, and her eyes fluttered wildly in her sockets, as though she was troubled by constant, terrible dreams. When, in a temporary state of wakefulness, two gentlemen of the Royal Society interviewed her, she told them about a hay field, about the flash of a doe's belly through the newly-turned rows, how the doe had gone to ground in a ditch, and Mary had watched her and — for a moment — felt herself akin to that creature, driven in fear from her home burrow when the mowers passed with their scythes. She described a terrible wildness of spirit, though the two gentleman were not clear if this was her own, or the doe's. Mary asked them: where was she now? Had she found her way back? She held onto their hands, as the tremors shook her belly. No one could answer her.

"Maternal Impression, a very definite case of it," one gentleman said. "We'll present it at the next meeting. Can you arrange for an inspection? Perhaps several — a number of our members will want to see it."

"Yes," said Daniel. "You tell us when and we'll have Mary ready. She'll like to hear so many people are interested."

Dr. Graves nodded sagely, and offered to let them read his recent treatise on the subject, as they withdrew, leaving Mary to her darkness, where — wriggling within her — the rabbits formed and died, formed and died, and she endured their birth and their return. In her half-waking state she saw not her husband, but a hulking and ancient devil who could not bear to see children born into the world, and so returned them to her after each bloody labor.

It was the landlady who found them out, when Margaret Toft visited the kitchen and asked her for a very small rabbit — dead or alive — the smallest she could find. When examined, Margaret wept and refused to speak. It was Daniel who admitted the deception and Mary Toft began her long, slow recovery.

The Monstrous Egg, Second Part

This is an ancient recipe, not so much invented, as rediscovered in eras of dread: the Terror, the Year of Five Emperors. It flickered in popularity after the Trinity Tests.

Take two dozen eggs. Take a pig's bladder, or a similarly round, water tight mold. From here, execution will vary by era and taste: do you prefer chicken or duck or ostrich? Do you prefer a wild boar's bladder or the more delicate skin-sack of a loveable piglet or a huge egg-shaped mold from a Tupperware party? Some recipes call for yolks and whites to be separated, the yolks set first in a spherical mold, then removed to the bladder, after which the whites are poured overtop and set in simmering water. These differences are cosmetic. What matters is the idea: the monstrous egg that, once cracked, spills its contents across the dining table.

(Monstrous Eggs can occur naturally, as was the case in 1862, in Antietam, when a languishing hen refused to lay. When butchered, she was revealed to be hoarding one of these creatures in her oviduct, so large it killed the hen.)

In the 1950s the Monstrous Egg appeared in the guise of a celebratory centerpiece for a summer buffet, recommended in at least one issue of *Women's Life Weekly* where it was sponsored by Jell-O and called the Delicious Gadget. The recipe required four packages of lime Jell-O cast in an egg-shaped mold, swirled with layers of sour cream and grated carrot, and, floating in its green depths, boiled eggs — the yolks like pupils — staring as they waited to spill like a secret onto an unsuspecting diner's plate. The recipe recommended a garnish of marshmallows.

In all cases, the appearance of such recipes prefigures a monstrous birth of another kind. That thing your hostess has placed at the center of the buffet, garlanded with marshmallows and water chestnuts? It is, in fact, the alchemical egg from which cracks the new and terrible world. No one knows if these eggs were ever eaten, or if they overwatched the table like the face of doom, l'oeuf monstrueux. The Delicious Gadget sits in the center of the suburban barbecue, awaiting detonation.

Mary Toft Had a Daughter

I have heard that there is, somewhere, a complex wherein these marvels, monsters, and prefigures are stored, or recorded, if their bodies have been destroyed. There are rooms full of jars in which float the pickled bodies of dog-headed children, and moon calves, and mouse-eared cats. Beyond these nameable creatures, there are stranger bodies, which seem to our eyes incompletely imagined, interrupted at some mid-stage of development, neither man nor beast nor angel. There are diagrams on the walls, and books of two-headed flowers and insects with thirteen wings, and other early attempts to record the marvel of conception as it intersects with history. There are, bodies stretched on pins in beds of wax, the remains of vivisected creatures, labeled by origins — mother and supposed father(s) — location, and date. The dates are significant: the children of plagues as well as comets find their resting places here; the children of Bikini Atoll, and the children of Trinity; the children of the Dutch famine of 1945, and children of the gulag.

It was to this secret archive — the Museum Clausum — that Mary Toft's surviving child was consigned by Dr. Graves's machinations. Graves was present at the terminal birth — before Daniel Toft confessed — and had whisked the little rabbit-daughter away when he found her among the refuse of half-rabbits that Daniel and Margaret Toft had pushed into the birth canal.

Mary Toft's daughter was a weak creature and smaller than the rest of her litter. The plan was for vivisection, so they might compare her anatomy to both rabbit and human models while still in action. At least two gentlemen of the Royal Society were eager to begin work, to slice open her belly and see, for a moment, her heart beat in the living air.

But rabbits are clever and their hearts are wild. Dr. Graves left the child on the hearth in the Museum's antechamber and held an impromptu meeting about who would author the resulting paper, and where they would seek publications, and what the book might be called when it was done.

While they spoke, the new thing — part Mary, part rabbit, product of a flash of light, conceived in the intersecting glances of woman and doe — escaped from her basket and onto the warm hearth. She smelled formaldehyde and vivisectionists, and though her eyes were newly opened, some knowledge must have been inherited by her infant mind, as though the circumstances of her birth had written into the code of her being a profound fear of men like Dr. Graves and his company.

She crept from hearth to door, a creature so tiny she might be missed, this palm-sized daughter, this rabbit-homunculus. Her skin was liver-colored, dark enough to fade into the carpet. When a latecomer opened the door, she hid rabbit-still in the shadows and saw her chance. She darted with all the speed of her wild mother. This was a happy ending: a second birth for Mary Toft's unnamed daughter.

A new creature quickens. A prefigure cracks the shell of the world: monstrous, miraculous, dog-headed, rabbit-bodied, conceived by the flash of a white belly in the dawn, the methylated DNA of a woman in duress, carrying her child through a famine or along a refugee trail from the flooded coast to higher land — from this crack will emerge something entirely new.

You might try to return it to its shell, but this time I do not think it will comply.

Acknowledgments

These stories were written with the support of the Ontario Arts Council.

They have also benefited from the insight of many editors, so I'd like to thank them first: Selena Middleton, CC Finlay, Neil Clarke, Ranylt Richildis, Ellen Datlow, Jaym Gates, E. Catherine Tobler, Michael J. DeLuca, Shannon Peavey, and Kelly Sandoval. I'd also like to thank the Clarion West class of 2015 for their contributions to "On Highway 18" in particular, and my short fiction in general. That includes our instructors: Andy Duncan, Eileen Gunn, Tobias Buckell, Cory Doctorow, and Nalo Hopkinson.

And because we never write alone, I thank all the friends and family who have talked through these stories with me: Sharron Campbell, Ian Campbell, Paulette Fitzgerald, Don Bourne, David Bourne, Jeff Strain, Dave Hickey, Sean Henry, Sarah Ervine Henry, Justin Key, Tegan More, and Christine Neulieb.

Thanks to all of you for the help.

About the Author

Rebecca Campbell is a Canadian writer of weird fiction. Her short stories have appeared in *The Year's Best Science Fiction, The Year's Best Science Fiction and Fantasy, The Year's Best Dark Fantasy and Horror,* and *The Best Science Fiction of the Year, Volumes 5 & 6.* She won the Sunburst award for short fiction in 2020 for "The Fourth Trimester is the Strangest," the Theodore Sturgeon Memorial Award in 2021 for "An Important Failure," and the Ursula Le Guin Prize for *Arboreality* in 2023.

You can find her online at whereishere.ca.

First Publication Credits

"The High Lonesome Frontier" was published on Tor.com in 2016.

"Lares Familiares 1981" was published in *Liminal Stories* in 2017.

"On Highway 18" was published in *The Magazine of Fantasy and Science Fiction* in 2017.

"The Other Shore" was published in *Genius Loci: Tales of the Spirits of Place* in 2016.

"Thank You For Your Patience" was published in *Reckoning Magazine* in 2020.

"The Bletted Woman" was published in *The Magazine of Fantasy and Science Fiction* in 2021.

"Such Thoughts are Unproductive" was published in *Clarkesworld Magazine* in 2019.

"An Incomplete Catalogue of Miraculous Births, or, Secrets of the Uterus Abscondita" was published in *Shimmer Magazine* in 2018.

YOU MAY ALSO LIKE

these Canadian titles from Stelliform Press!

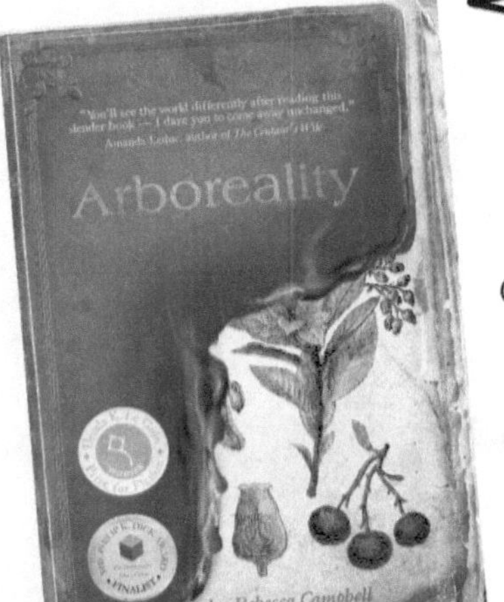

Winner of the 2023 Ursula K. Le Guin Prize for Fiction, Rebecca Campbell's Arboreality is a novella in short stories about what it takes to survive and thrive in a climate changed world.

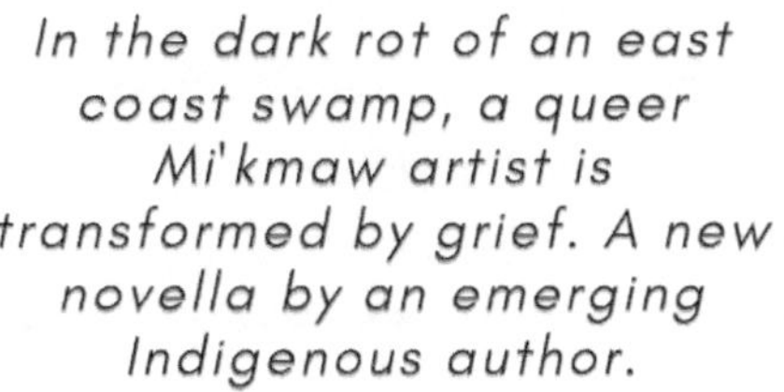

In the dark rot of an east coast swamp, a queer Mi'kmaw artist is transformed by grief. A new novella by an emerging Indigenous author.

**Earth-focused fiction. Stellar stories.
Stelliform.press.**

Stelliform Press is shaping conversations about our climate changed world and our place within it. We invite you to join the conversation by leaving a comment or review on your favorite social media platform. Find us on the web at www.stelliform.press and on Mastodon, Bluesky, Instagram, Facebook, and Threads @StelliformPress.